# WRITING UNDER FIRE
## POETRY AND PROSE FROM UKRAINE AND THE BLACK COUNTRY

# Writing under Fire
## Poetry and Prose from Ukraine and the Black Country

Edited by
Sebastian Groes, Carmel Doohan,
Sofiya Filonenko and Kerry Hadley-Pryce

London
*Jet*stone
2024

A *Jet*stone paperback original.

ISBN 9781910858271

The right of the individual contributors to be identified as authors and translators in this work has been asserted in accordance with the Copyright, Designs and Patents Act, 1988.

© The contributors, 2024.
All rights reserved.

All unauthorised reproduction is hereby prohibited. This work is protected by law. It should not be duplicated or distributed, in whole or in part, by any means whatsoever, without the prior permission of the Publisher.

Cover photograph by Tessa Posthuma de Boer.

Cover design by Hannibal.

CONTENTS

| | |
|---|---|
| Introduction | 9 |
| A Brief Introduction to the Literary History of Ukraine Vitaly Chernetsky | 24 |
| The Tale of the Sirens Tetiana Belimova | 35 |
| Stories We Tell To Children Carmel Doohan | 43 |
| Poems Dmytro Semchyshyn | 54 |
| Výbačte Casey Bailey | 59 |
| The Thirteenth Month of 2022 Bogdan Kolomiychuk | 60 |
| May You Have Mountains of Melons Niall Griffiths | 70 |
| Distant Bird V Formations Rostyslav Melnykiv | 74 |
| Hackle R. M. Francis | 80 |
| The Grey Coat of Silt Ivan Andrusiak | 81 |
| In Grey Countries Not So Far From Here Anthony Cartwright | 84 |
| Bloodied Earth Liudmyla Taran | 88 |
| Bloodied Earth Kerry Hadley-Pryce | 92 |
| When You Grow Up Roksolana Zharkova | 95 |
| Poems Kuli Kohli | 97 |
| Poems Ihor Pavlyuk | 99 |
| The People-Eater of Leningrad Sebastian Groes | 108 |

| | |
|---|---|
| **Poems** Halyna Kruk | 113 |
| **Speaking in New Tongues** Roy McFarlane | 121 |
| **Flour and Lies** Liudmyla Taran | 123 |
| **Mother Becomes Daughter Becomes** Charley Barnes | 133 |
| **Last Poems** Victoria Amelina | 134 |
| Notes on the Contributors | 137 |
| Acknowledgements | 145 |

*In memoriam*
Victoria Amelina (Вікторія Амеліна)
1986-2023

INTRODUCTION

The Russian invasion of Ukraine on 24 February 2022 has plunged Ukrainian citizens into an unceasing nightmare of terror and horror. It was also a shock to the wider world. Let's start with some facts. The annexation of the Crimea by Russia between 2014 and the end of the first year of the invasion costs the lives of 4,400 Ukrainian forces, 6,500 Russian forces and 3,404 civilian lives, according to the UN. The total number of troops killed or wounded since the Russian invasion in 2022 is a staggering 500,000, including 300,000 Russian troops, according to the *New York Times*. Thousands of Ukrainian civilians have died and over 8 million people have been displaced.[1] Between 1 May to 26 June 2023, Russia fired 35 ballistic missiles, 320 cruise missiles and over 550 Shahed-136s, which are so-called loitering munition kamikaze drones (produced by Iran) – many of which were intercepted by Ukrainian forces (aided by the west).[2] Ukraine has destroyed about half of Russia's 2329 tanks. US officials estimated that Russian fire at the start of the war was around 20,000 artillery rounds per day, which has recently plummeted due to ammunition shortages. These staggering numbers capture coldly the destructive fire of war, of death, blood, pain, trauma – and they unveil the incendiary madness of this senseless, fratricidal war.

How to comprehend such unimaginable statistics? How can we

---

[1] Helene Cooper *et al.*, 'Troop Deaths and Injuries in Ukraine War Near 500,000, U.S. Officials Say', *New York Times*, 18 August 2023. See: https://www.nytimes.com/2023/08/18/us/politics/ukraine-russia-war-casualties.html (accessed 16 December 2023).

[2] Ian Williams, 'Russia Isn't Going to Run out of Missiles', Centre for Strategic and International Studies, 28 June 2023. See: https://www.csis.org/analysis/russia-isnt-going-run-out-missiles (accessed 16 December 2023).

start to fathom such stark information? The sheer numbers are mindboggling, incomprehensible.

Literature is a particularly good way of making sense of these seemingly unfathomable statistics. This book hopes to offer a small contribution to understand the terror that Russia is inflicting on the neighbouring, independent state to its west. *Writing under Fire* offers words and words alone, but they are words that contain carefully crafted fragments of clarity and wisdom that respond to military fire power. The contributions contained in these pages write back in protest against the inhumanity of what is being done to a sovereign people.

The title of this anthology refers unambiguously to the horrific situation that many writers in Ukraine find themselves in: writing at a time of an unwanted, futile war, and writing *about* the Russian invasion and the bloody, traumatic consequences that it is having on their country and fellow citizens. The book's title situates this project in a much longer history of war writing; literature that reflects on and often protests against war, producing responses to, for instance, the poetry of the First World War, the Spanish Civil War, World War Two and the Vietnam War. Yet the genre is as old as human history, as Ihor Pavlyuk sadly concludes: 'Human history,/Unfortunately, is war'. Though it is said that war writing is always late, with the most definitive responses coming long after a war has ended, the title of this collection is also about the act of writing *during* wartime – the importance of and need to capture the human experience in all its detail at the time of crisis: the anger and frustration; the exhaustion and sleepless nights; the deafening sirens announcing bomb attacks; the panic when rushing to a grubby bomb shelter with a child tucked under one's arm; the painful train journey to a safer place as one is forced to leave one's home; the loss of family members or friends. It is important that writers employ the tools they have at their disposal – an exceptional level of expression; a highly developed critical acuity; and symbols, metaphors and other stylistic devices – to capture human experience at a time of grave crisis. Indeed, this book's starting point is that literature – even in a time when it has intense competition from other media – continues to have an important role to play in setting down our lived experience because it comes closest to capturing human consciousness.

There is another layer to the title of this collection: Ukrainian writers are living at a time when bullets and missiles can and will kill them. They write in fear and anger, aware that their future lives and writing could be wiped out at any moment, as happened to one of our contributors. Victoria Amelina was a young, talented writer who on 27 June 2023 was injured by a Russian missile attack whilst having dinner in a pizzeria in Kramatorsk. Victoria died on 1 July. She was only 37 and, just before her untimely death, she had received a residency in Paris and was considering moving to France with her 12-year-old son. Victoria's death symbolises everything that is so objectionable about war in general and this war specifically: a young, intelligent and sensitive life snuffed out for nothing. We are here publishing three poems by Victoria, one of which is darkly ironic. 'A Poem About The Poet's Death' meditates without any romanticism on the vagaries of a writer's life, especially during wartime. This book is also dedicated to Victoria's memory.

This project started with a collaboration that Professor Sofiya Filenenko (at that point Professor of English Literature at Berdyansk State Pedagogical University as well as Honorary Professor in the Humanities at the University of Wolverhampton) and Professor Sebastian Groes (Professor of English Literature at the University of Wolverhampton) embarked upon a couple of years ago. The University of Wolverhampton's School of Humanities supported staff and students of the English Department at Berdyansk State Pedagogical University through various teaching and research activities. In November 2022, Sofiya and Bas organised a Being Human Festival event at which students, staff and authors read works from the English canon, as well as their own work, to which writers from the Black Country responded. The creation of a literary bridge between our two countries continued to develop, and soon the editors, joined by Kerry Hadley-Pryce (Lecturer at the University of Wolverhampton) and Carmel Doohan (Writer in Residence at the University of Wolverhampton), compiled a list of ten Ukrainian writers who would produce work to which ten writers from the Black Country would respond. This dialogic approach is no easy feat and the reader will see how the conversations between the writers unfolds in various forms of engagement. Sometimes the British writers link tangentially with other work or respond to poetry with prose, at other times we find more direct, intimate conversations such as the one between Bogdan Kolomiychuk's Facebook journal and Niall Griffiths' response.

One goal of this project is to raise money to replenish the stock of Ukrainian (university) libraries, many of which were looted and set on fire by Russian soldiers. All contributors have waived fees and/or remuneration for their work in this book. But we also hope that this book will stimulate the intellectual life of Ukraine as well as grow the reading culture in the country. Indeed, if one sought an expression for what this book might do, one can find it in the following image in Liudmyla Taran's short story 'Flour and Lies':

> Halyna has filled her windows with piles of books. A good reason to have collected them, it turns out. The windows are criss-crossed with tape and stacked with their spines. Perhaps this is what prayer would look like if it were made visible.

Books as protection from outside danger, books as insulation, books as a request for help or expression of gratitude – books literally as a window onto the world. Throughout these pieces you will find moments of thanks to books and the comfort and sensations they bring. As Kolomniychuk notes in passing, 'We miss books desperately, even though we wouldn't have a lot of time to read them. I could find no room in my backpack for my trusted Kindle. Now I regret it.' The uses, value and appreciation of books and reading are underscored and highlighted by the war precisely because of their absence or by people's inability to read because of the disruption caused by the war.

### Sirens and Heroes

This book was nearly called *Sirens*. Throughout this collection it will be impossible for the reader to not hear shrieking air-raid alarms going off. In the opening story by Tetiana Belimova, shrieking sirens urge a mother to rush her children to a bomb shelter, and in the frontline Facebook diary by writer/soldier Bogdan Kolomiychuk to reflect on the ubiquitous presence of sirens: 'And when the alarm sounds, the choice is very real: run to cover or finish eating this ambrosia. Take the melon and run, you would say.' And as Ihor Pavlyuk writes in his poem 'Sirens and Bells': 'These are not the sirens/That once awaited Odysseus./ [...] These sirens are different...'

Yet all writers here also evoke a significant doubling of 'sirens', referring to the literal sirens that announce potential death from above but also making a connection with the myths about Orpheus, who survived a dangerous encounter with the Sirens by playing his lyre, as well as Odysseus, whose crew put bees' wax in their ears to protect them from Sirenic seductions.

As the reader will also see, many other figures from especially Greek mythological traditions make their way into these pages: Cerberus; Hercules; Jason and the Golden Fleece; Icarus; the Gorgon; Circe; Penelope; Cyclops. You will also encounter the Cossack Mamai, the mythical figure of the Ukrainian warrior and folkloric hero, which has a long history in art and literature, and is usually depicted with a *kobza*, an instrument resembling a lute that symbolises the Ukrainian spirit. So, it seems that the war has awakened or certainly intensified a deep, mythological consciousness, a mindset that many of us (thought we had) lost in an era dominated by scientific and technological revolutions that engender a forensic, rational gaze. The writers here seem to fall back onto these ancient stories for support – and for making sense of their present experience of terror and confusion.

Many of the pieces bring back a certain kind of depth of consciousness that is imaginative but also temporal. They remind us of a cyclicity of time – or what Nietzsche called the 'eternal return', the idea that time and events, including war, repeat themselves over and over (as Pavlyuk suggests above). Counterintuitively, the writers here also seem to find a certain comfort in this idea. The allusions to the mythological past create an imaginary archaeology that resonates in a different kind of spiritual digging, including an excavation of cultural deep history. For instance, in Dmytro Semchyshyn's poem 'resurrection' a local excavation of a German settlement unearths a broken clock as well as a small figurine of Jesus – offering the potential of Ukraine's rebirth after this current episode of darkness – yet Semchyshyn's unsettling conclusion for Ukrainians is that any possible rebirth is blocked, at least for the time being.

Implicit in this collection's reference to Greek (demi-)Gods is the fact that the Ukrainian people have been forced against their will or wish into the role of hero in its modern definition. On the one hand, there are the men who fight on the frontline – and many of them are civilian soldiers: next to professional military officers, Zelensky's government called up engineers, carpenters, waiters, firefighters and students.[3] On the other hand, we have 'ordinary' civilians who have been thrust into the role of soldier or volunteer who fundraise or provide drones, heating, used cars, tactical medication and personal body armour. Members of the volunteering group Free Spirit have 'provided over 400 vehicles, 75 communications devices like Starlink receivers and satellite phones, 13 tons of batteries and generators, 60 portable power stations, a handful of reconnaissance drones, and over 100 tons of basic necessities like food, cots, mattresses, and clothing.'[4] We also need to think of the journalists, writers, scientists, publishers, translators and university lecturers who have continued to do their work in extremely trying circumstances. *Writing under Fire* is a tribute to the Ukrainian people and their tenacity.

### Women's Perspectives on the War

Though some of the contributions are written by active soldiers such as writer Bogdan Kolomijchuk, the reader will also see that this book does not offer only dispatches from the frontline. The contents are incredibly diverse – on many levels. We see, for instance, a wide variety of genres in these twenty-one pieces: poetry, prose, but literary genres including folklore and fairy tales, which Anthony Cartwright and Sebastian Groes turn to. We also encounter many different modes, including, for instance, Kerry Hadley-Pryce's lyrical response that pays homage to T. S. Eliot's 'The Love Song of J. Alfred

---

[3] Yasmeen Serhan, 'Ukraine's Civilian Soldiers', *The Atlantic*, 11 February 2022; at https://www.theatlantic.com/international/archive/2022/02/russia-ukraine-conflict-civilian-forces/622048/ (accessed 3 December 2023).

[4] See Jake Steckler, 'Why Ukraine's Civilian Volunteers Are the Unsung Heroes of the War', *Time*, 2 August 2023; at https://time.com/6300653/why-ukraine-civilian-volunteers-matter/ (accessed 2 December 2023).

Prufrock' (1915). Importantly, half of the contributions here are written by women, which gives this collection an important slant on the impact of warfare. *Written under Fire* shows how war not only violently disrupts the experience of men who fight at the front, but also how it impacts on other arenas, including social relationships and family life. In the opening story, Tetiana Belimova tells us not only how she needs to flee with her children to a bomb shelter, but we also see how she and her children need to say goodbye to her husband when they are offered a safe haven in Poland – a heart-breaking ending full of uncertainty. These contributions offer an analysis of the war's impact through explorations of emotion and affect, captured through form and style and also thought, imagery and symbolism.

The refocusing of perspectives on the war in this manner accords with a recent turn in literary production as well as its critical responses. One may think of *Women's Fiction and Post-9/11 Contexts* (2015), which showed how women's writing responded in subtly different ways to the infamous terrorist attack, or Caroline Magennis' *Northern Irish Writing after the Troubles* (2021). Both focus partly on the ways in which women approach conflict situations at the level of form and content. For instance, Halyna Kruk shows how war disrupts domestic life:

> in our home dangerous objects were always
> hidden from children […]
> but who could have known how much danger there is
> in an ordinary cast iron bathtub hanging above your head,
> the collapsed wall of the living room, the nail from a painting
> that holds in place the neighbours' apartment's ceiling
> who could have known how heavy
> the packed bookshelves can be, how hard the upholstered
> furniture can be, our home is unreliable, our home is above an
>     abyss

Such descriptions aptly communicate how a supposedly safe, solid space can become a dangerous trap, dragging its inhabitants down vertiginously into an unknown void.

In Liudmyla Taran's 'Flour and Lies' a daughter is taking care of her frail, elderly mother who has barely survived a heart attack. In this tender story told in intimate free indirect speech, the daughter meditates on the ways in which her 'ordinary' domestic chores, including the washing of her mother's hair, gain new significance. When the protagonist needs to say goodbye to her daughter, who is fleeing their city for a safer place, what would have been an everyday parting becomes infused with meaning: 'The door creaks as they shut it behind them; a small cry like an orphan thing. It has never made such a noise before.' In these minute observations we see how literature can capture the unreal nature of war-torn life whilst suggesting how the particular perspectives offered by women supplement our understanding of the war. A special concern lies with children's experience: as a classic symbol of hope and the future, in the war context young children are especially important. Yet again the figure of the child is no longer straightforward. In Roksolana Zharkova's poem 'When You Grow Up' there hangs a great sense of unease over the future: 'Tell me, child,/Will there be anyone who will love us, so rootless/Who will love us, so rootless and so unblooming?' Indeed, the speaker of the poem is entirely unsure of the future: 'Next year new fruit will sprout and bloom,/But who will want to harvest them?' In Ivan Andrusiak's poetry the natural cyclicity of the seasons itself has come to a halt – a most unnatural effect of this futile, hopeless war upon the world.

## Reality under Fire

When exploring the pieces in *Writing under Fire*, the reader will come to understand many writers connect the war in Ukraine to other kinds of crises dominating our contemporary experience. One of the biggest crises that inhibits any immediate prospect of resolution of the Russian war on Ukraine is introduced by mis- and disinformation. The fake news war has become an important phenomenon of the increasing polarisation and stand-off between Russia (along with what was once called the 'axis of evil') and the west. This divide between Russia and more progressive forces is an important object of discussion in this book. Many of its key questions are to do with how individual people and groups feel themselves in possession (or not) of a shared sense of reality.

It is clear that Russia censors journalists (its own as well as foreign, such as Marina Ovsyannikova, who protested against the spread of fake news by the Russian military on live TV) whilst attempting to infect the perception on virtual platforms of the Russian aggression against Ukraine.[5] Although it might be easy for many of us in the west to see how a dictatorial regime attempts to brainwash its populus, the actual consequences are less easy to combat. The Thomas Theorem offers a framework for thinking about this. This theory, elaborated by sociologists William Isaac and Dorothy Swaine Thomas in 1928, states that if people define situations as real they are real in their consequences. It does not matter if a belief is 'right' or 'wrong'; perceptions, and the experience of them as true, grow stronger the more people believe them. Reality is, of course, subjective, perceptual and endlessly interpretable: it is, and becomes, what we believe it to be, both individually and collectively.

And yet, as Niall Griffiths notes in his response to Kolomijchuk, 'This journal is your truth, Bogdan, and this is THE truth; a concept become alien now. Objective reality is a notion to be debated, a mutable idea, but not for you; you see and recognise and know lies.' This is how we may characterise the 'crisis of the real' as a result of the recent rise of mis- and disinformation in the digital sphere – although there is nothing new about it. It is not so much whether we believe that the Covid-19 pandemic was related to Bill Gates's 5G roll-out or that Russia has not committed any war crimes in Ukraine. But the undeniable fact is that we perceive our realities to be more and more fragmented, perhaps irreconcilably so. The question of who owns reality – and how one might reclaim a sense of ownership over life when war cuts the ground from beneath your feet? – are at the heart of this book. These questions are complex and they seek to understand the current forms of polarisation that complicate this war.

Needless to say, though, the war reality is irreducible and undeniable. As all the Ukrainian pieces herein testify, war's disturbing immediacy is most urgently and violently felt. Liudmyla Taran notes

---

[5] See, for instance, Mark Scott, '"Grotesque" Russian disinfo campaign mimics Western news websites to sow dissent,' *Politico*, 27 September 2022; at https://www.politico.eu/article/russia-influence-ukraine-fake-news/ (accessed 3 June 2023).

in her story: 'On the twenty-fourth of February, in the twenty second year of the twenty-first century, Kyiv shuddered with explosions. [...] This could only be a nightmare. But it wasn't. This was war.' Kolomijchuk also reports the irreducible reality of war: 'Slashed trees, burned machinery, ruined houses. Sometimes I am surprised when my eye finds something solid and unharmed. Such is my present reality.' Yet at the same time the routine 'reality' of everyday life is torn to shreds by the way: there is something unreal about the war experience – a nightmare from which Ukrainians are trying to wake up. As Halyna Kruk writes, there is a certain surreal and implausible feeling to the disrupted reality of war:

> Lack of a logical motive, explain to me, say you, why are they killing us,
> There must be some motivation, some reason.
> They don't construct plots in books this way.

Ihor Pavlyuk also notes that the war situation is as 'if common sense is forever blocked by a blood clot.' In short, if the world were a brain, we have suffered a collective stroke that impairs our thinking and behaviour. And this impact of the state of emergency goes even further, eating away writers' ability to express themselves coherently. Victoria Amelina noted the crippling effect that war has on her craft:

> It's just the war reality
> devouring all punctuation
> devouring the plot coherence
> devouring coherence
> devouring
> As if shells hit language
> the debris from language
> may look like poems
> But they are not

We, in the west, do not have direct access to this actuality. We have mediated versions of the violence of war which we experience through the many screens by which we surround ourselves. We are genuinely shocked and truly upset, powerless to intervene, like an audience in a

Greek tragedy. Yet we also know that we do not know. We are lucky. We are fortunate. We live in a relatively safe environment with a generally stable system of governance that we may take for granted. In this context, *Writing under Fire* is an attempt to bring home the experience of war that our Ukrainian friends are going through, a bid to communicate the suffering and anguish by means of the literary imagination.

We can read and view journalistic, factual reports of the war on our screens every day – these are important to keep us informed of the military, political and humanitarian developments of the ongoing horrors and trauma. But they are far from enough: what the news does not give us in any depth are dispatches on the war's impact on human consciousness; on the trauma that cripples people's mental states and impacts their emotions; on the heart-wrenching decisions that 'ordinary' citizens are faced with – having to say goodbye to your husband not knowing if you will ever see him again; being forced to leave your home and home country for refuge in a different country, culture, language. These pieces show us what war feels like *on the inside*.

### Connecting Ukraine and the Black Country

We should note that the Black Country literary tradition has a distinct connection to thinking about such issues. The Black Country is, after all, a peculiar landscape, an 'interfacial rim',[6] uncelebrated and little acknowledged. Its reputation as borderless and its identification through geographical contradictions, which in turn are based in geology would seem to offer possibilities of what Edensor calls 'phantasmagoric experiences' related to creativity.[7] Many Black Country writers (Anthony Cartwright, specifically) use their writing of fiction as a method of conveying more than simply a story, and

---

[6] Marion Shoard, (2002:117). 'Edgelands', in S. Jenkins (ed.), *Remaking the Landscape: The Changing Face of Britain* (London: Profile Books, 2002), p. 117.

[7] Tim Edensor, 'Mundane Hauntings: commuting through the phantasmagoric working-class spaces of Manchester, England.' *Cultural Geographies* 15 (2008), p. 329.

instead walk a thin line between fiction and non-fiction. Patricia Leavy's work into fiction as research seems particularly pertinent here: 'Who is to say their works are "just" fiction, or social research. Might they be both at once?'[8]

Ukrainian literature and literature from the Black Country have some things in common. Despite their obvious difference in size and geographical location, both literatures emerge from border zones, from disputed territories, produced by authors with fractured identities and shifting, often split cultural heritages. As Vitaly Chernetsky outlines in his introduction to Ukrainian literature in this volume, Ukrainian writers are frequently deemed to belong to Russian (post-)Soviet literature, but only because of their colonial situation – which forced them to imbibe the Russian language – though the actual socio-cultural and political situation is infinitely more complicated. Some writers have a split ethnic background but are claimed for Russian literature because they speak Russian. This is why the Ukrainian writer Volodymyr Rafeyenko, for instance, recently decided to give up the Russian language and learn to read, speak and write Ukrainian.[9] This is a politico-economic act as Russia continues to dominate and (re-)colonise Ukraine and other former Soviet republics through various ideological measures – and outright warfare.

Ukrainian identity is fraught and still in the process of wrenching itself loose from its colonial ties. To understand the complex heritage, the case of T. S. Eliot comes to mind: does the US-born poet, who lived most of his life in England, belong to the American or to the English canon? Or, perhaps an even better example is someone like Joseph Conrad: Józef Teodor Konrad Korzeniowski was born in Berdychiv, Ukraine, then part of the Russian Empire, though the region had once been part of the Crown of the Kingdom of Poland. Conrad would become celebrated as one of the greatest writers in

---

[8] Patricia Leavy, 'Fiction and the Feminist Academic Novel.' Qualitative Inquiry 18, 6 (2012), pp. 518-9.
[9] Luke Harding, 'Hearing Russian brings me pain': how war has changed Ukrainian literature', The Guardian, 4 October 2023. See https://www.theguardian.com/world/2023/oct/04/russian-language-war-ukrainian-literature (accessed 4 October 2023).

English – which was his third language (he learned to speak it fluently only in his twenties). He can be said to write in a specific tongue but not to belong exclusively to a certain national literature or culture. Perhaps we should assign Conrad to the European canon. Within this context, there may be a case to be made for including some Ukrainian literature in this European tradition.

The Black Country similarly struggles with its various heritages. According to Edward Chitham, 'The Black Country never completely discards the past'.[10] And it was an American Diplomat, Elihu Burritt, who came to the area in the 1860s and coined the phrase: 'The Black Country, black by day and red by night, cannot be matched, for vast and varied production, by any other space of equal radius on the surface of the globe.'[11] The Black Country, located in the West Midlands of the UK, is considered the cradle of the industrial revolution. Because of this, its resources – coal, sand and limestone for instance – were plundered, and its geographical location in the Midlands was strengthened by the building of road and canal networks. Townships tended to rely on the prize of their geology to form identities through trades. For example, the mining of iron ore, limestone, sandstone and Etruria Marl in various locations led to manufacturing specialisms: steel works in Dudley and Brierley Hill, glassmaking in Amblecote and Stourbridge, lock-making in Wolverhampton, nail-making in Netherton and Cradley, and brickmaking in Pensnett. The emphasis on manufacturing – doing and making – and excavating mines in order to provide the resources resulted in a physical 'working class' of Black Country people: producers, makers. Work was physically hard, over long hours, often dangerous. The very ambition of the place, the tenacity of its people, resulted in a kind of external and internal pollution, of both the air and of health. Dialects (both in terms of word choice, accent and intonation) were (and some might consider still remain) inextricably linked to the poor air and the hangover of the individual trades carried out in each township. But the sense of Black Country identity in the aftermath of the industrial revolution became as unclear as its cartography.

---

[10] Edward Chitham, *The Black Country* (London: Longman, 1972), p. 11.
[11] Elihu Burritt, *Walks in the Black Country and its Green Border-Land* (London: Sampson Low and Marston, 1868), p. 1.

Ukraine and the Black Country have more things in common including the nature of their economy and their relationship to power. Ukraine is the key producer of wheat for Europe – the yellow-blue colour of the Ukraine flag represents golden fields of grain under a clear blue sky – playing a perhaps somewhat humble role *vis-à-vis* European economic power. For the Black Country, the decline in manufacturing industries and consequent boom in service industries, resulting in loss of job security, has changed its economic landscape. Such comparisons establish a common ground that puts the two places into a potentially dialogic relationship.

### Contra spem spero - Against All Hope I Hope

This book is not a systematic anthology nor a comprehensive encyclopaedia of contemporary Ukrainian writing. It is an ad hoc, relatively random, on-the-run and under-fire project that depended on the availability of writers who are living in a country under siege; hiding in bomb shelters; fulfilling duties on the front line; living as refugees in foreign countries; or were on trains or planes fleeing their home country. They wrote their pieces in fear of their own and others' lives; worried about their children and their future; filled with rage against Russia and Putin.

The collection is consequently dark, brooding and sombre. It contains trauma, displacement, mourning, suffering, blood and death. *Writing under Fire* has been written at a time of war and the texts are awash with images of bloodied earth, ruins and exit wounds. It is fuming with hopelessness and hatred, but at the same time it also longs for the Ukrainians not to be crippled mentally by their hatred. Liudmiyla Taran states, 'Wash the knives, beat the earth clean/of the blood and hatred.' Many of the pieces here are full of despair, and its authors sometimes are on the brink of giving up – and losing all faith. Ihor Pavliuk writes: 'I, disappointed in humanity, have grown small,/Like a child under a bombardment without a mother' and 'I had thought – humanity is wiser…/Now my songs are quieter –'.

This gloomy fatalism captures the wider sensibility of our early twenty-first century world. It is perhaps no wonder that the disappointment and regret we get in these pages are connected to a wider sense of crisis that is technological, political, socio-economical and ecological. Aren't we all tired of the fact that the world and humanity won't change its ways? Aren't we sick of being stuck on this ship of fools?

Yet, ultimately this is a book that offers a glimmer of hope in desperate times. It is about creating a perspective onto the present situation with a view to placing these horrible events in a long history whilst looking towards a different, brighter future in times to come. In the midst of the front-line horror, Kolomiychuk creates some relief through often humorous observations of unexpected events and ideas. He finds solace in small human gestures.

As Dmytro Semchyshyn notes about his poem 'resurrection', 'I suppose this poem is one of the most desperate texts I have ever written. According to it, the Earth really seems a pest house. Nevertheless, I haven't lost my hope yet.' Roksolana Zharkova's eyes are also pointed to the future, longing for a simple pleasure that makes life beautiful, which is mirrored by Kerry Hadley-Pryce's contribution that imagines a future point in time when the narrator undertakes a walk of the Black Country with our Ukrainian friends. Kuli Kohli too meditates on the future: understanding that our future in Britain is compromised when our allies, our friends longing for freedom and democracy, are under siege. Indeed Hadley-Pryce and Kohli use the pronoun 'we' to suggest that we are in this war together and that we will make it through together.

We must not be naïve about what literature can achieve: we cannot simply 'rewrite' the terrible situation that Ukraine finds itself in nor can we make the Russians give up with a beautiful, moving poem. Yet this book underscores the power of words to contribute to changing people's perceptions and minds. It starts from the firm be conviction that the role of art and literature should not be underestimated in this time of crisis. Artistic, imaginative storytelling is a way of creating an angle on the world that helps us to work through traumatic events. These stories and poems give voice to suffering but together they also create a literary bridge whereby different people and cultures come together to find solace.

Indeed, literature is affirmed as indispensable in Halyna Kruk's poem 'Dnipro, 14 January 2023':

> Literature lives on with this cry in your ears,
> with this hand and this slipper,
> knowing what was behind them in reality's unblurred version,
> the version not softened by AI.
> This is what literature has always been for.

And despite the hardship and bleakness, the eyes are tentatively turned towards the future, a post-conflict situation – which will eventually come. One of the most famous Ukrainian poems is 'Contra spem spero' – which translates as something like 'Against all hope I hope', a source of inspiration and solace in times of crisis. The final stanza of the poem goes as follows:

> Yes, I will smile through my tears
> Sing my songs through evil and adversity,
> Hopeless, a steadfast hope forever keeping,
> I shall live! Away with thoughts of grief!

The writers here also write in this spirit and look towards the future – to a point at which we can rejoice and celebrate together in a safer world. We leave you to enjoy the contributions in this collection and will end with the words of Niall Griffiths, who in his response to Kolomiychuk provides us with an image of a better, brighter future for Ukraine: 'Such is what the future could be. [...] My greatest hope is that I, we, the world, will be gifted with more of your words. [...] Love and luck and gratitude to you.'

Amsterdam/Wolverhampton/Lviv
December 2023

## A Brief Introduction to the Literary History of Ukraine
Vitaly Chernetsky

For a long time Ukraine was primarily associated with its depiction by outsiders, especially in the two rival regional powers that exercised considerable influence upon it, namely Poland and Russia. But it has a rich literary history of its own.

As with other nations, its folklore is a separate story; the tradition was passed down orally for centuries and began to be studied and transcribed in earnest only in the nineteenth century. (Those ancient texts can feel very modern, as in the case of the spring song 'Shum', a pre-Christian text recorded in the 1850s that was transformed into a hit song at the 2021 Eurovision contest.) However, the written tradition also reaches far back. The medieval literature of the state of Rus (later called Kyivan Rus, as Kyiv was its capital) flourished especially from the tenth to the early thirteenth centuries, but ended with the Mongol invasion. Its relation to later Ukrainian culture can be comparable to that of Old English writing before the Norman conquest.

Written culture of the thirteenth to seventeenth centuries was primarily associated with the church; just as in Eco's *The Name of the Rose*, monasteries were the main centres of literature and learning. While Ukraine did not have a fully-fledged experience of the Renaissance, its culture, including literature, flourished during the Baroque era. This is also when it got its first modern universities, which became new centres of secular writing, including poetry and drama. The seventeenth century also marked the beginning of Muscovite imperial expansion in Ukraine, and many educated Ukrainians influenced the newly developing secular Russian literature of the late seventeenth/early eighteenth century. Given Ukraine's status as a stateless nation then (and for much of its history), many of its authors composed in multiple languages besides the Baroque-era early Ukrainian (most notably in Latin and Polish, and later in Russian). This stage of the Ukrainian written language is closer to the modern one but is still hard for us to follow now, so it can be likened to Chaucer's Middle English.

The pinnacle of this Baroque-era writing is associated with the poet and philosopher Hryhorii Skovoroda (1722-1794). From a modern vantage point we could describe him as something like an eighteenth-century version of a hippie or a New Age guru. After an eventful career as a choir singer, university instructor, and even a wine procurer for the imperial court, he wandered on foot from place to place for the last twenty-five years of his life, often staying as a guest of local gentry who sought his wisdom. He is best known for his series of Socratic dialogues and a poetry collection, *A Garden of Divine Songs*, which in his lifetime circulated widely in manuscript.

In 1798, just a few years after Skovoroda's passing, a major event happened that radically changed the course of Ukrainian literature: the publication of *The Aeneid* by Ivan Kotliarevsky (1769-1838), a mock epic retelling of Virgil in which the main characters, including the Greek gods, are described as characters from Ukrainian folk life. This was the first work of literature written in vernacular Ukrainian, and afterwards it was this idiom that won out as the standard for literary Ukrainian used to this day. Kotliarevsky's book was much loved by a wide variety of readers for its vivid imagery, great sense of humour, and the clear delight you can sense from the author savouring the language riches of Ukrainian. It started a boom in Ukrainian-language writing, but also produced a problem. Since this was a comedic work, Kotliarevsky's followers primarily engaged in comedic literary forms, inadvertently creating a prejudicial belief that Ukrainian was fit only for humorous entertainment. To counter this, a pioneering Ukrainian prose writer, Hryhorii Kvitka-Osnov'ianenko, wrote his novel *Marusia* (1834), explicitly aiming to prove that one could meaningfully and successfully engage with serious and lofty emotional topics in Ukrainian as well.

However, in that era many writers of Ukrainian origin, for a variety of reasons, ended up writing in Russian; for some, Ukrainian was a language for local use, and Russian became a means to address a wider audience. The best-known writer from this group is Mykola

Hohol, a.k.a. Nikolai Gogol (1809-1852), whose Ukrainian-themed works written in the 1830s became a huge success first in Russia and then internationally.

Ukraine found its great national poet, Taras Shevchenko (1814-1861), within a few short years after *Marusia*'s publication. He began writing poetry in 1837 and published his first collection in 1840; with it, any talk of Ukrainian language not being fit for the widest variety of civic, philosophical, or any other topics became moot. Shevchenko came from very humble origins, born a serf and orphaned at a young age. His talent as a visual artist was discovered before his recognition as a poet. A group of supporters bought him out of serfdom and helped him enroll in the Academy of Fine Arts in St. Petersburg. In the mid-1840s he was able to return to Ukraine as a free man and became part of a group of free-thinkers known as the Cyrillo-Methodian Brotherhood. His poetry from the mid-1840s is highly ambitious and in many ways ahead of its time. Thus his poem 'Caucasus' (1845) is a pioneering articulation of the solidarity of the colonized across national and religious divides of a kind not seen elsewhere in European poetry of the time. Shevchenko and other members of the brotherhood were arrested in 1847; his punishment was particularly harsh, as he was sent to serve as a common soldier, with a strict ban on writing and drawing personally imposed by the Tsar. Ten years of harsh exile ruined his health; amnestied in 1857, he was able to return to St. Petersburg, resume writing great poetry, and be widely lauded, but sadly he passed away too soon. One of his close friends and peers, Panteleimon Kulish (1819-1897) authored the first Walter Scottian historical novel in Ukrainian, *The Black Council* (written mid-1840s, published 1857); he also founded the first Ukrainian literary journal, *Osnova* (1861-62) and later translated both Shakespeare and the Bible into modern Ukrainian.

The success of the Ukrainian literary revival and the hardening political climate in Russia led to a radical curtailment of possibilities for Ukrainian-language publications. A partial ban was imposed in 1863, and a virtually complete ban on publishing anything in Ukrainian followed in 1876, to be lifted only during the first Russian revolution in 1905. However, a relatively small but culturally important part of Ukraine after the partitions of the Polish-Lithuanian Commonwealth ended up under Austrian rule, and that part was where free publishing in Ukrainian was possible, and thus, while before 1863 its role in Ukrainian cultural growth was modest, in the new circumstances it rose to be viewed as the Piedmont of Ukraine's hope for a Risorgimento. Additionally, with Mykhailo Drahomanov, a major intellectual who became a political émigré, Ukraine got another outlet for censorship-free publications in the West, including a series of literary almanacs he published in Geneva.

The leading literary figure of western Ukraine under Austrian rule was Ivan Franko (1856-1916), an extraordinarily active and prolific author of poetry, prose, drama, and scholarly writings. He is often considered the second most important Ukrainian writer after Shevchenko. Alongside him, several younger authors gradually came to prominence. While Franko stayed primarily focused on realist writing and social problems, his younger peers became more engaged in a modernist search for new forms and new means of expression to reflect the radically changing world. Their ranks included the brilliant proto-expressionist short story writer Vasyl Stefanyk (1871-1936) and the Nietzsche-influenced feminist prose writer Olha Kobylianska (1863-1942). In the Russian-ruled part of Ukraine, Drahomanov's niece Larysa Kosach gained fame under her pern-name Lesia Ukraïnka (1871-1913). A poet and playwright, she is usually considered the third greatest Ukrainian writer; her major work includes a bold modernist reinterpretation of folkloric themes in *A Forest Song* (1911), a feminist polemical rejoinder to *The Iliad* in her *Cassandra* (1907), and a similarly powerful feminist reinterpretation of the Don Juan motif in her play *The Stone Host* (1912). Olha Kobylianska and Lesia Ukraïnka, both suffering from ill health, met only a couple of times, but they left a passionate, long-lasting correspondence that can be considered one of the greatest love stories by letter in world culture.

Another friend of Lesia Ukraïnka, Ahatanhel Krymsky (1871-1942), a prominent Orientalist scholar, was also a pioneering writer, exploring homoeroticism and gay male subjectivity in his poetry and prose, the earliest of it dating to the 1890s. The novel *Andrii Lahovsky* is one of Krymsky's greatest achievements. Its first two parts appeared in 1905, but the full text was only published in 1972.

A prominent early modernist not to be missed is Mykhailo Kotsiubynsky (1864-1913), whose short stories and novellas mark him as a pioneer of impressionist writing and, alternatively, as an author with great psychological depth. His novella *Shadows of Forgotten Ancestors* attained global fame thanks to its cinematic adaptation by Sergei Paradzhanov, released in 1965, which many consider the greatest work of Ukrainian cinema.

Volodymyr Vynnychenko (1880-1951) may be better know now as a leftist politician and one of the leaders of independent Ukraine in 1917-1920 who later lived in exile, but he was also a significant prose writer and playwright, who combined in his works a fresh modern diction with interest in the rapidly modernizing society. His plays garnered considerable success on European stages and, before his works were banned in the Soviet-ruled part of Ukraine in the 1930s, he enjoyed the status of Ukraine's most popular and best-read contemporary author.

The 1910s marked the debut of three major Ukrainian poets. Mykhail Semenko (1892-1937) was the founder and leader of Ukrainian futurism, a fascinating national school of the global avant-garde movement; tragically, he was among the many Ukrainian writers who perished during the Stalinist terror. The lives of the two other key Modernist poets of this generation, Pavlo Tychyna (1891-1967) and Maksym Rylsky (1895-1964), were spared in the terror; they, alongside the younger Mykola Bazhan (1904-1983), came to be known as the 'captive generals' of Ukrainian poetry; however, the work they produced after 1933 did not match the power and innovativeness of their younger literary selves.

The years between the collapse of the Russian empire in 1917 and the imposition of Stalinist repression and terror in the early 1930s witnessed a prodigious flourishing of Ukrainian art and culture along all forms and genres, literature being no exception. The schools and movements were too numerous to list here. A clear leader of the Ukrainian literary world of that era was Mykola Khvylovyi (1893-1933), who began as a poet but came to major fame as prose writer and essayist. His suicide in response to arrests of fellow writers marked the symbolic end of the period that later came to be known as the Executed Renaissance. Hundreds of talents were tragically lost early, like the promising novelist Valerian Pidmohylny (1901-1937). His first novel *The City* (1928) is a captivating portrayal of Kyiv in its dynamic transformation in the 1920s.

With the repressions in Soviet Ukraine, the spotlight and opportunity for innovation again shifted to the western part of Ukraine, especially to the regions that after 1921 found themselves under Polish rule. The brightest literary star of that period is Bohdan-Ihor Antonych (1909-1937), an original Modernist poet lost too soon (he died because of unsuccessful surgery).

With the Stalinist repressions resuming with renewed vigour after World War II, the centre of innovation shifted to the refugee community in the DP camps in the Western allies' occupation zones in Germany. In these challenging circumstances, cultural life nevertheless flourished. Among its leading figures I would first name V. Domontovych (pen name of Viktor Petrov, 1894-1969), who began his literary career in the late 1920s. Petrov mysteriously disappeared in 1949 only to re-emerge in the Soviet Union a few years later; he was apparently deeply undercover as a Soviet spy, but no traces of those duties can plausibly be found in his fiction and essays published in the 1940s, such as the novel *Dr. Seraphicus* (begun in the 1920s, published 1947). Other prominent figures in that revival are the poet and translator Ihor Kostetsky (1913-1983), the poet and prose writer Yuri Kosach (1908-1990, Lesia Ukraïnka's nephew), and the essayist Yuri Sherekh (pen name of the linguist George Shevelov, 1908-2002). The camps were closed in the early 1950s, and this new diaspora scattered across Europe, North and South America, and Australia, but the impulse created then continued.

A new generation of diasporic authors who experienced World War II and the DP camps as teens came to prominence in the 1950s/early 1960s. Several of them were associated with the New York Group of Ukrainian poets, most notably Bohdan Boichuk (1927-2017), Bohdan Rubchak (1935-2018), and Yuriy Tarnawsky (b. 1934). Tarnawsky is the leading diasporic Ukrainian author writing in both Ukrainian and English. A fascinating associate of the group who charted an independent path is the poet and prose writer Emma Andiievska (b. 1931); her work is boldly experimental and strongly influenced by surrealism and other schools of thought engaging with the oneiric and the unconscious.

With the end of Stalinism and the start of the so-called Thaw in the Soviet Union, a new generation of writers tried to express themselves more openly. In contrast to the more avant-garde orientated writers in the diaspora, their work is more traditional in form but aimed to push the limits of what was permitted by censorship. In poetry, the leading figures were Lina Kostenko (b. 1930), Vasyl Symonenko (1935-1963), and Ivan Drach (1936-2018); in prose, Hryhir Tiutiunnyk (1931-1980). The greatest literary figure of that generation is a visionary late Modernist poet and fearless political dissident, Vasyl Stus (1938-1985) who perished in a prison camp when Gorbachev was already in power. His poetry, intense in its philosophical explorations and richness of vocabulary, deserves to be appreciated alongside the globe's leading literary figures of his generation; fortunately, a comprehensive translation project is now in the works.

The 1970s marked a new era of repression; while less severe than in the 1930s, it nevertheless destroyed the lives of many talented folks, like the poet Hrytsko Chubai (1949-1982). Some, like the noted magic realist novelist Valerii Shevchuk (b. 1939), wrote their works 'for the drawer', publishing them once censorship began relaxing in the 1980s.

The 1980s for Ukraine were marked by both excitement and trauma. The Chornobyl nuclear accident of 1986 deeply scarred the nation's psyche, and this was reflected in literature as well (Tamara Hundorova, Ukraine's leading contemporary literary critic, aptly dubbed the wave of postmodernist Ukrainian writing of the 1990s 'the post-Chornobyl library'). Yet the political liberalization and the eventual collapse of the Soviet Union also brought unheard-of freedoms. A young generation of writers was eager to champion and explore this contradictory condition and fight the ossified culture of official Soviet Ukrainian literature. Its unquestionable leaders were two poets who later also became active as prose writers, Yuri Andrukhovych and Oksana Zabuzhko (both b. 1960); they continue producing important and powerful new work to this day. Andrukhovych, together with two other poets, Viktor Neborak and Oleksandr Irvanets (both b. 1961), formed an experimental poetry group named Bu-Ba-Bu, whose carnivalesque public performances became one of the hallmarks of change in the late 1980s/early 1990s.

The renewed independence of Ukraine achieved in 1991 brought a lot of excitement but also a lot of challenges, unprecedented freedoms alongside a deep economic crisis. Literary development witnessed a great diversity of voices, representing the country's many different regions, cultural leanings, and linguistic diversity. Serhiy Zhadan (b. 1974), a native of the Luhansk region in Ukraine's far east, came to be recognized as the leading author of his generation, first as a poet, later also as a prose writer. Overall, contemporary Ukrainian writing brings us an expansive spectrum of themes and a continuing generation of new meanings and new breakthroughs. The Revolution of Dignity of the winter 2013-2014 and Russia's war against Ukraine that soon followed have had a transformative impact on Ukrainian culture, which only intensified with Russia's full-scale invasion unleashed in February 2022. There has been great trauma and suffering, but also a lot of resilience and beauty. There is a lot of intense, powerful poetry, ambitious prose, and innovative in-your-face drama coming from the pen of Ukrainian authors today. I encourage you to seek it out; you won't be disappointed.

WRITING UNDER FIRE
POETRY AND PROSE FROM
UKRAINE AND THE BLACK COUNTRY

THE TALE OF THE SIRENS [1]
Tetiana Belimova


'Mum, why are they so loud?'

At the entrance to the bomb shelter stands a young man with sad, droopy eyes and a fag in his mouth. Silently I think of him as Cerberus. I run into him every time the children and I go down to the shelter where he seemingly always keeps the watch at the door – our guard dog. Strangely, he never goes inside the shelter. Perhaps he is claustrophobic or wants to be able to keep smoking.

I pick up my youngest, Varia. The oldest, Sonia, marches along leading our little dog, Roki, who whines and resists. He hates the shelter and its smells. It's full of people, and it's hard to find a place to sit. It's also very stuffy. The lights glow dim and high, doing little to light this sad place. I continually have the feeling that all of this is happening to other people, not to us. Is this just a dream? Am I going to wake up in a moment and find, with great relief, that everything I'd just seen was a figment of my imagination?

Finally, we find a bit of space by a wall. I roll out the yoga mat. Sonia throws down two pillows and a quilt. The frightened dog relaxes a little and climbs into her lap. We sit.

'Mum, why are the sirens so loud?' asks Varia.

She has her arms around my neck, making it hard for me to breathe. But I can't loosen her embrace, not yet. I can feel her heart

---

[1] This story is dedicated to the victims of the Russian terrorist act in the city of Dnipro on 14 January 2023, which took the lives of forty-five Ukrainians, six of them children. Twenty people are still considered missing.

beating inside her like a frightened bird; I can see how large her pupils are. I need to tell her something interesting, something that will captivate her and prevent this fear from taking root in her soul. I think of the beautiful book of Greek Myths that I bought for the girls last Christmas. It has a myriad of secrets and discoveries inside; a feather from Icarus' wing in a special envelope, the Cyclops' eye that rolls out from a secret pocket. It has been our favourite for months.

'You remember the Sirens, right? You remember our book about them?'

Her arms on my neck relax a little.

'I don't remember...'

She is tricking me into telling her again about those half-women, half-fishes of the sea who lured Ulysses and his mates into a trap and wanted to kill and eat them. But Ulysses already knew about their wicked nature. He followed advice from Circe, the witch, and ordered all his men to plug their ears with wax. But Ulysses did not plug up his own ears. Instead, he tied himself to the mast of the ship and insisted that his men did not let him escape. He wanted not only to hear the song, but to withstand it.

A tight circle of listeners forms around us. Someone pulls up a folding chair they have prudently brought from home. Someone else asks me to tell the story louder. An older lady offers my children mint candy to help with nausea.

We come out of the bomb shelter, and it is still early. The sirens are quiet now, waiting for the next enemy strike. Sometimes I think the sirens must be installed right in the middle of the lake next to our apartment building. Otherwise, how do you explain the fact that the alarm is a hundred times louder here, near the water? We decide not to go home yet but take the dog for a walk and stay for a while at the playground. While my daughters take turns on the slide, I check my phone and read about Odessa.

'Mum, why are you crying?'

I draw in a full chest of air and look into my elder daughter's unchildlike eyes. Today, on 23 April 2022, while we were sitting in the bomb shelter, a Russian rocket killed three generations of women in an Odessa apartment: a three-month old baby girl, her mum and their grandmother.

'I'm just…'

I wonder if my eight-year-old is mature enough to take in and comprehend this news. Or would it be better if I said nothing? I do everything I can to preserve her and her sister's childhood world. And, like every mum, I want to protect my children against the catastrophic reality of war. But I am only human. Should I – can I – really plug my girls' ears with wax so they won't hear the wailing of the sirens and the news of other children's deaths?

'I'm just feeling tired today…'

I first heard about the Sirens when I was a child. My mum used to subscribe to a children's magazine for me, and each issue of Малятко retold one Greek myth. I have clear memories of reading about the deeds of Hercules; about Jason and the Golden Fleece; about the Gorgon; and about the Sirens. Even back then, these sea monsters prompted never-ending questions. Why were the Sirens so bloodthirsty and intent on sinking ships? Why were they so treacherous to the sailors who trusted their voices? And why was their magical talent combined with such a beastly nature that demanded human sacrifice?

It's been a long time since I was that child studying pictures in a children's magazine. My fascination with the mermaids of the sea is far in the past, but since 24 February 2022, these other sirens – with their low wail or high shrieking – have become an everyday part of most people's lives in Ukraine. These other sirens are impossible to get used to. Every time you hear them sing, you want to turn into a beetle and hide in the smallest crack. To just stay alive, just survive, here and now, on this planet that has opened a mouth of war and is threatening to eat you alive. Not all of the Earth wants to destroy you, of course, but the country that takes up a sixth of the globe's surface does.

I didn't hear the sirens much at first. Before the war, my family lived in a comparatively new residential area in Kyiv. This neighbourhood was not equipped with air-raid sirens. On the left bank of the Dnipro river, Poznyaki had everything – a tube line straight to the city centre, comfortable apartment blocks with wonderful playgrounds, schools and nurseries, a variety of supermarkets, beauty salons, and gyms, even movie theatres, restaurants, and cafes – but no sirens. At first, we downloaded an app to our phones from Google Play, and when an air-raid alert came they buzzed and whined. That was a 'soft' version of the real sirens that would soon be installed everywhere to announce the threat from the sky.

They wailed so loudly, there was nowhere to hide from them. Their pitch reminded you that there was no safety where you lived: if a rocket hit your building, you would not survive. We learned the 'two-walls rule', which told us that the safest place in a building is where there are at least two walls without a window between yourself and the street. In theory, the first wall would absorb the blast and the second the shrapnel. However, despite this rule, you would most likely be buried under the total weight of concrete, brick, dry-wall, windows, doors, furniture, and possessions. Your bathroom would kill you fast, stab you with shards of tile or mirror. The doorway would hold the weight of the floors above you only momentarily, or maybe not at all, and would fold you under it. Your home, full of all the things you have carefully chosen and arranged, would become your trap. You had five minutes, a mere five minutes, to grab your go-bag, dress your children, put the dog on the leash and dash down the stairs (not using the lift – another obvious death trap in an air-raid). Then you had to run over to the nearby building where a bomb shelter had been set up and where Cerberus would wait for you, always…

I sit down next to my husband in the kitchen. We watch the news on TV. Again and again it shows a beautiful Odessa apartment building with a hole where the entrance should be. My husband has come home late. The tube did not run for half the day while the air-raid alert was on, and the number of people waiting for it kept growing. It was a challenge even to get down to the platform, let alone on a train. My husband concentrates on moving the sour cream around in his plate of borsch. He has no desire to eat but, at the same time, he doesn't want to hurt my feelings and will of course eat everything I put on the table. Eventually, that's what happens. While I'm clearing the dishes, he calls out to me, 'We'll go to your mum's dacha for the weekend. Get a chance to relax in the country.'

But he is wrong.

He doesn't know it yet, but a loud siren, louder even than the ones in Kyiv, has been installed in the small village where my parents have bought their little dacha. This siren does not wail like the ones in the city but seems to moan on a single note, like a large, wounded animal.

The evening we arrive, our neighbour from across the street stops by.

'Why aren't you covering your windows? I can see yours from the other end of the village. Everything's supposed to be blacked-out!'

The neighbour is upset with us because we have brought a certain carelessness from Kyiv, an unwelcome attitude. In small spaces great events always manifest themselves in greater relief. The village around us is almost empty of the men we used to know – they have all been taken to the front.

'We'll close the curtains right away. We just forgot.'

The village is pitch black, lit only by the stars high above us, indifferent to our troubles, to the war that has stained Ukraine's map red with occupied territories. For the stars, we are not even the microbes we wish we could turn into every time there's an air-raid. From the point of view of the universe, we must be nothing.

The next day, my eldest and I go to the end of the street where Grandma Nadya lives. Grandma Nadya has always kept a cow, and every summer, when we came to the village, we bought milk from her. Now, the path to the homestead is overgrown with grass. There's a padlock on the gate in the fence. The neighbour next door tells us that when the war started, Grandma Nadya's daughter came from Poland and took her there. They sold the cow and locked the house.

On the way back to Kyiv, I turn up the radio in the car. These rules will save your life. The announcer's pleasant voice calmly and confidently delivers instructions on what to do when you find yourself buried in a collapsed building:

Do not panic
Try to free your arms
Clear the space around you
Prop up what's left of the ceiling with something strong
Keep calling for the help which is most certainly coming

I find myself memorising these instructions verbatim, as if they were a poem.

Another anxious week goes by. I finish my online lectures and send my students the exam questions. The department Head phones to ask me to come to the university. He has an important message that he wants to deliver in person, so we agree to meet the following day.

Sonia does school online and Varia's nursery has closed and I don't have anyone to leave them with. The Head is waiting for me in his office. He takes off his glasses and gives me and my daughters a fatherly look. He is struggling, and I can guess why; he is about to hurt me. He tells me that no guest-lecture hours are scheduled for the next academic year. I do regret this so much, he says. The country is at war, he adds, as if I had somehow failed to notice. Funding and next year's enrolment figures are unpredictable, he tells me. No one can predict how many upper-class students who have left the country will stay abroad and not return. I nod. Of course. I understand. We spend some time chatting about new books that have been published despite the war and about Ukrainian publishers who are fighting heroically for their industry's survival. We talk about the weather. Then, he glances at the clock above my head. He is expected at a department Heads' meeting. I walk to the tube with my girls, and the eldest asks me again why I am crying. This time, I tell her the truth.

That night, we watch the news in the kitchen. My husband is eating supper, while I sit next to him with my laptop. I look for fellowship offers abroad in my subject area. Many universities in Europe want to support Ukrainian scholars and fund their studies. I choose some to apply for in the morning and close my laptop.

We wake up in the night to the wailing. It is after four. Sonia runs in and buries herself under our blanket. Varia arrives a few minutes later, followed by Roki. They are all convinced that next to us – the grown-ups – they are somehow safe. The siren keeps wailing, but I am frozen. I can't make myself get out of my warm bed or make everyone run to the bomb shelter in the other building. My daughters breathe evenly at my sides. What has happened to my will to survive? The girls fall asleep the instant the siren stops wailing and my husband seems to be dozing off too. I look out of the window and see a red blob slowly appearing on the horizon. The sun still rises despite it all.

'What are you doing?'

Sonia is leaning on my shoulder and studying the words on my laptop screen. She can't put them together into sentences yet: her English is basic, appropriate to her eight-year-old mind.

'I am writing a research proposal,' I say, and start explaining it before she can ask her next question. 'I want to study how people's perceptions of certain words and phrases have changed. Words like "sirens", "air-raid", and "bomb shelter".'

'The sirens are wicked! Why study them?' she asks. 'They were wicked monsters before when they used to kill people on the seas. And now they are wicked too, because they kill people with bombs!'

'They are not wicked, and not monsters,' I try to explain. 'They raise the alarm when the enemy planes carry rockets to Ukraine. You see? They want to warn everyone about the danger. That's why they wail. And my research is not about the sirens exactly. It's about war.'

'Why should anyone study war?'

'I want other people to know what war is like and what we, the Ukrainians, had to go through. I want them to know about the Russian crimes. They are the real monsters, not the sirens.'

'You mean they are not people but monsters, like in our book of myths?'

How would I have answered such a question before the war? But now I think about it for only an instant.

'Yes.' I realise that I have no doubt about this. 'Yes. The Russians who drop bombs and launch rockets at our cities are monsters.'

We go out to buy ice-cream. When we are standing in the check-out line the air-raid alarm sounds. The polite voice on the loudspeaker rises over the siren to request that everyone proceed to the shelter in the underground parking garage immediately. We leave our shopping in the trolley and go downstairs.

'I got an answer from Jagiellonian University, Poland! They want to support my project with a six-month fellowship!'

My husband says he is happy for me, and I believe him. I know that he has long wanted me and the girls to leave Ukraine. He promises to take care of my baby tomato plants and reassures me that it won't be for long. Tears roll down my cheeks like large peas, leaving wet splodges on my T-shirt. He hugs me. He promises again not to forget to water the plants in our apartment. I tell him I don't want to go without him. We've never been apart for such a long time. We stand there, embracing, rocking a little in unison, moved by a rhythm only the two of us can feel. The day is ending, and the dusk stretches its cobwebs across the wall. A palpable gloaming fills the room but neither of us notices and turns on the light. Perhaps it's better this way. We're still under black-out orders.

I clasp our passports. We leave the Lviv railway station and board the train to Krakow. Ahead of us is the border and the customs control. The train is crowded with women and children. However different we are in our habits, family pictures and memories, we are all made similar in our grief. Some believe, as I do, that we will be able to return to Ukraine very soon, while others intend to look for a new home far away from our country's insane neighbour to the North.

The train stops at the border. Only two or three hundred metres separate us, Ukrainian refugees now, from Poland, which will be our new home for the duration of the war. Suddenly the sirens sing out again, as if mourning those leaving their home country. Are they calling us back? If someone decided to hold a funeral for faith in humanity, this is what the march would sound like. But my faith is still alive. I know the exceptions only prove the rules. I still have faith in people's kindness. I believe I will come back home. I believe the sirens do not cry in vain and will save some lives. Then, finally, the air-raid alert is over, and the train inches forward – into an unknown future.

Theissenegg, Austria<br>
10-18 January 2023

Translated by Nina Murray

## Stories We Tell To Children
Carmel Doohan

The second most common flag in the village where I live is the Derbyshire one. Its bright green cross on a pale blue background flies outside pubs and in front gardens. In early 2022, the most common flag became the colours of Ukraine. As well as being hung in windows and shop fronts, it was raised on a flagpole in the park. Blue and yellow bunting hung over the entrance to the school and blue and yellow ribbon was wound around the gates of my daughter's nursery.

My daughter, Molly, learned about death not through the war in Ukraine, but from the death of the Queen. In June 2022, red, royal blue and white ribbon was temporarily added to the yellow and blue on the railings, as she celebrated the Queen's platinum jubilee. We baked red, blue and white fairy cakes and she made a picture of the Queen from a paper plate, glitter and gold paint. A few months later, in September, the Queen died.

For days, the radio spoke of nothing but her death. Molly was fascinated by the days of queues of people waiting to look at this old woman's dead body. Before the Queen there had been a cat, perfectly intact, but dead, at the side of the road, and before that a neighbour's dog – but it was the Queen that got her asking questions. She was nearly three and death itself began to fascinate. She wanted to walk through the graveyard that surrounds our village church and read all the names. They all died because they were very old and had finished their lives, she told me: I had obviously pulled my punches when I explained how death worked.

In my defence, I didn't do heaven. I told her that our bodies went into the earth, and that the energy left in them helped the trees and plants grow. She seemed to like this idea. Two months after the death of the Queen, giant red plastic poppies and life-size rusted metal silhouettes of soldiers covered the hill above the village playground. This is how she learned of war. When she asked what they had been fighting about, I said that it was mostly land and power, and that men from our village had died in that war. I told her that they were made to dig holes in the mud and live in them, shooting at the soldiers living in mud on the other side. When she asked about the red flowers I said that the dead bodies had helped the flowers to grow, and where the fighting had been there were now fields and fields of poppies. I don't know if this is really true. It was something someone told me when I was a child.

Molly began to listen more carefully to the radio in the kitchen. When it spoke of war, she wanted to know more about it. Listening to BBC Radio 4 with a three-year-old is a great way to face your own geopolitical ignorance, along with your woolly beliefs and susceptibility to propaganda. Molly started to talk about Ukraine and ask why they were fighting. Land and power again, I told her. Russia, the country next to Ukraine, wants to control its people and their land. *What are they talking about now?* she would ask as presenters, politicians and pundits discussed strikes, the cost of living, war and the overheating climate. *Why are they saying that?*

We watched *Paddington* together for the first time in March 2022. Everyone's favourite asylum seeker crossing the sea in a small boat with only marmalade to eat. Putting aside the talking-bear-in-hat element, the timing invited the film to carry additional notes of the absurd. The Caribbean calypso song – 'London is the place for me' – that accompanies Paddington as he searches for a home in Notting Hill, was written by Trinidadian musician Aldwyn Roberts, who came to Britain aboard The Empire Windrush. He performed the song for news crews in 1948 as his fellow passengers disembarked to begin a new life in Britain. As we watched, the Windrush report on the progress made following the 2018 scandal had just been released, finding that there had been 'a lack of tangible progress or drive to achieve the cultural changes required' to protect and respect the diaspora being celebrated through this music. To compound the absurdity, I then read that in the Ukrainian version of the film, Paddington Bear is voiced by President Vladimir Zelensky himself.

In response to Russia's full scale attack on his country, Zelensky had just addressed the UK parliament via Zoom, delivering a powerful and astutely-pitched Churchillian address: 'We will fight until the end, at sea and in the air. We will continue fighting for our land, whatever the cost. We will fight in the forests, in the fields, on the shores and in the streets...' He received a standing ovation and the UK Prime Minister, Boris Johnson, gave a return address with similar overtones: 'When my country faced the threat of invasion during the Second World War, the British people showed such unity and resolve that we remember our time of greatest peril as our finest hour. This is Ukraine's finest hour.'

Later that March, Liz Truss, then Foreign Secretary, further reinforced the alignment of British identity with that of Ukraine: 'Putin's illegal, unprovoked invasion of Ukraine has shattered the notion that freedom is free. Our two nations understand how precious freedom is, and what it means to fight for it. This is exactly what British foreign policy is. We stand up to bullies. We fight for freedom. We have a history of standing up to dictators. We should be proud of our country, and our long-standing commitment to freedom and democracy.' Her subsequent, and somewhat abrupt, segway – 'Now is the time to end the culture of self-doubt. The constant self-questioning and introspection. These ludicrous debates about statues' – ended on a defiant note: 'Our history – warts and all – makes us what we are today.'

*Our history, warts and all.* A hundred years prior this speech, in early 1922, the British Empire was at its height: it covered a quarter of the earth's land and ruled over 458 million people. In the February of 1922, following decades of exploitation, brutal repression and control, and after protracted and bloody wars, Egypt would overcome an occupying imperial force to win independence. Later that year, Ireland too would start to end hundreds of years of brutal English colonial rule by forming The Irish Free State.

Part of Ukraine's response to Putin's annexation of Crimea was the passing of a series of laws on decommunisation. These laws banned 'the promotion of the symbols of communist and national socialist totalitarian regimes' with a penalty of up to five years' imprisonment. The Soviet Union – of which Ukraine was part from 1919-1991 – was recognised as a criminal and terrorist regime. As a Kyiv city deputy put it: 'Finally, there is an understanding that our colonial heritage must be destroyed.'

Banned images and flags included the hammer and sickle, which until then had taken pride of place on a shield carried by the Soldier of the Motherland monument outside Kyiv's National Museum. Along with the Soviet flag, images of Mao, Lenin and, somewhat incongruously, Che Guevara were also banned. Yet as some images disappeared from public view, others proliferated: a yellow fist on a blue background – the symbol of the right-wing ethnic nationalist Svoboda party – and the black and red flag of the UPA, the nationalist Ukrainian Insurgent Army. There is controversy and complexity surrounding this flag. To some, it shows a commitment to Ukrainian national identity, its perseverance, sovereignty and strength; to others, it has strong associations with twentieth-century nationalist pogroms, paramilitary groups and the World War II era nationalist leader Stepan Bandera.

Bandera occupies a polarising role in Ukrainian society, at once freedom-fighting hero and fascist, Nazi collaborator. While ordinary people fought for their lives and the survival of their loved ones, new stories and ideologies moved in to replace the old, one officially sanctioned history replacing another. By 2016, 51,493 Ukrainian streets and 987 cities and villages had been renamed and 1,320 Lenin monuments had been removed. In 2018 Stephan Bandera's birthday was declared a national holiday, and new statues were erected in his honour.

Histories and interpretations layer over one another in a tangle of flags. Factions multiply, both nationally and behind enemy lines, each using history, and particularly that of the Second World War, to deprecate the other. When I first began to read about the situation in Ukraine, I found myself wondering, why this obsession with World War II?

Then, as I read, I started to look at my own country, still caught in its endless obsession with Brexit, and as I watched it begin a process of blue-and-yellowification, I saw that we too have a similar obsession.

*We stand up to bullies. We fight for freedom. We have a history of standing up to dictators.* Our politicians and newspapers continually called upon the British 'Blitz spirit' to deliver Brexit and fight coronavirus, but the British history of World War II is, of course, more complicated than that.

In June 2020, as part of the Black Lives Matter protests, a statue of Churchill in Parliament Square had 'Churchill Was A Racist' sprayed across it. In response to this, Boris Johnson said, 'The statue of Winston Churchill in Parliament Square is a permanent reminder of his achievement in saving this country – and the whole of Europe – from a fascist and racist tyranny. We cannot now try to edit or censor our past. We cannot pretend to have a different history.'

A few days later, on *Good Morning Britain*, Professor Kehinde Andrews, Director of the Centre for Critical Social Research at Birmingham City University, gave a different view: 'I think Churchill did some good, certainly. But let's be honest, Sir Winston Churchill was responsible for the deaths of millions of black and brown people. Churchill *was* a eugenicist. In fact, Churchill and Adolf Hitler would have probably agreed on many things when it comes to race.' When the host of the programme told him that to equate Churchill to Hitler and the Nazis is deeply offensive, he replied: 'It is not deeply offensive. University College London – where they will be taking down statues soon – supported eugenics. Sir Winston Churchill believed in eugenics, and those beliefs which led to the extermination of the Jews are similar to the views which led to enslavement. They came from the same place.'

Only days before this, the statue of slave owner and philanthropist, Edward Colston, was toppled and thrown into the River Avon in central Bristol. Dramatic visions of statues toppling is something I remember seeing on TV as a child in the years after the fall of the Berlin Wall: Lenin's giant head lowered by a crane in East Berlin in 1991; Lenin falling, arm outstretched, pope-like, in Vilnius, Lithuania, a few months later. It was something the other side did, something that sits alongside evocations of the End of History. Yet, as Lenin statues toppled in Ukraine and the war raged, it became apparent that this particular End of History – the gloating defeat of communism; the Washington Consensus-led economic shock therapy; the arguable overreach of NATO – is still playing out. History, it seems, doesn't end, it just changes its statues.

★

I write this in July 2023, while slowly reading Caroline Elkins' new book, *Legacy of Violence: A History of the British Empire*, about another ideologically-enforced end of history – a British one. In the 1960s British colonialism was being dismantled: 'The union jack was lowered and flags of new nations were raised in ceremony after ceremony. Cyprus (1960); Nigeria (1960); Sierra Leone (1961); Tanzania (1961); Uganda (1962); Jamaica (1962); Zanzibar (1963); Malawi (1964); Zambia (1964); Malta (1964); The Gambia (1965).' Elkins' book offers meticulous details of how our empire operated, how liberal and paternalist propaganda was used to justify racist and supremacist action, and how the 'colonial clause' added to the European Convention on Human Rights allowed it to disregard the convention – essentially legalising lawlessness – in its colonies. Newly discovered documents show the enormity of the bonfire of secrets occurring at the end of empire, giving specifics to stories of smoke from the burning of evidence hanging over Delhi, and over Nairobi, for weeks after independence was celebrated. The documents show detailed official instructions to turn to ash anything that 'might cause embarrassment to her majesty's government', and to ensure that 'papers which are likely to be interpreted, either reasonably or by malice, as indicating racial prejudice or religious bias on the part of Her Majesty's government' were 'packed in weighted crates and dumped in very deep and current-free water at maximum practicable distance from the coast in the sea'.

As the Maidan uprising was gathering pace in Ukraine, largely unremarked upon here in Britain, the editing and erasures of our own End of History, fifty years before, were being stirred up. Thousands of hidden files, 'discovered' in a 'migrated archive', were being haltingly made accessible to the public. This was, as Ian Cobain writes in *The History Thieves*, 'an extraordinarily ambitious act of history theft, one that spanned the globe, with countless colonial papers being incinerated or dumped at sea [...] Thousands more files were spirited away from the colonies and hidden for decades in a high security intelligence facility in the south east of England.' This facility was Hanslope Park, Buckinghamshire, where, after repeated legal requests arising from a reparations trial brought by torture survivors of the Kenyan Mau Mau massacre, thousands of previously undisclosed documents were suddenly 'discovered'. Millions more withheld files, said to cover more than fifteen miles of floor to ceiling shelving, that should have been available under public records acts, also came to light during this period, many covering the period of the troubles in Northern Ireland.

The famous lines from *Nineteen Eighty-Four* – 'every record has been destroyed or falsified (...) every statue and street and building has been renamed, every date has been altered. And that process is continuing day by day and minute by minute. History has stopped' – come to mind, and in May this year there was indeed some controversy over which society George Orwell was satirising. Maria Zakharova, a top Moscow diplomat, declared that the novel was not a satire about Nazi socialism and Stalinist totalitarianism, but about British liberalism. While there is something ironic about a Putin supporter making this claim – what Orwell was primarily satirising was the spread of disinformation and the twisting of language to suit the purposes of propaganda – we must acknowledge that the dystopia of a history continually rewritten to suit those in power critiques not only the Soviet Union but Orwell's own country too.

What we do, do not, and must not equate in history is always significant. A decision to equate Communism with Nazism, declaring both to be terrorist and criminal regimes, was upheld in 2019 by Ukraine's constitutional court and in response, Putin signed an opposing law, criminalising any public attempt to equate those same regimes. While our state passing legislation about how history must be understood and spoken about still falls into the realm of what 'other countries do', the ideological rewriting of history is in no way something that only happens in elsewhere. Caroline Elkins' horribly detailed tome, describing hundreds of years of systemic murder, extraction, imprisonment and massacre under the guise of liberal imperialism, implicitly reinforces the assertions Kehinde Andrews made on Breakfast TV. Based on ideas put forward over seventy years ago by Hannah Arendt and Aimé Césaire, he later expanded on his comments and offered an unpopular equation about our own history of WWII: 'The British Empire lasted far longer, did more damage, and in many ways paved the way for the Nazis and their genocidal ideology. We do no favours to the victims of the Holocaust by pretending otherwise. If we forget the past we are likely to repeat it.'

★

When I first began thinking about this essay, the surreal image that came to me was of Father Christmas hanging on a crucifix in a department store in Japan. The familiar turned upside down and inside out. I remembered it as an anecdote told by Slavov Žižek, but the problem was, when I looked it up, I couldn't find any details; such an event might have happened in 1930s Tokyo, or perhaps Kyoto, or it could just be an urban myth. Despite this, as I try to understand the dissonances in my country's response to the situation in Ukraine, I keep returning to this image, and the way it allows the full incomprehensibility of our own ideological mix to be suddenly revealed.

While I failed to find verifiable facts about the department store anecdote, I did, however, find something that Žižek said about Father Christmas that feels even more relevant. He takes the belief in Santa as a way to illustrate his theory of 'belief through others': parents pretend to believe in Santa on behalf of their children, while children pretend to believe in Santa on behalf of their parents. Is our patriotism, or our belief that our nation is one of the 'good guys', a similar loop of wishful thinking?

Our governments incongruously united and officially sanctioned support of Ukraine feels like something more than a show of solidarity with those bravely fighting for their lives. We – on both the left and the right – have pulled Ukraine into our history wars, our culture wars. We send missiles and ammunition and we shine blue and yellow lights on Number Ten and Big Ben. We paint our buses with the word UKraine and we hang flags outside our schools. Are some of us, in identifying not with the empire-hungry Russia – bringer of tyranny, imperialism and brutal repression – but instead, with the ex-Soviet colony bravely fighting for independence and democracy, trying to rewrite history?

As I cook Molly's dinner and we listen to the radio, she asks more questions about what she hears. I want to answer her questions with the honesty she deserves. The Houses of Parliament lit up, their coloured reflection shimmering in the Thames, feels like a blue-and-yellow washing of our national story. It is the new mythologies we built as we emerged from the Second World War that allow us to fall into this strange overidentification with Ukraine. As the colonies that had fought alongside the allies in the war won independence one after another, we transformed our image: we built an 'Island Story', one in which we were the plucky underdog, the outsiders who had prevailed against fascism alone in Churchill's 'people's war'. As the war ended and India won independence, we quietly shed the millions of colonial and ex-colonial subjects who had fought alongside us from the story, and, as historian David Edgerton puts it in *The Rise and Fall of the British Nation*, 'a new nation was forged in the battle of Britain and the Blitz'.

As the war escalates, I read the coverage about the fighting and the refugees, and our responses to those refugees. One image, in *The Guardian*, shocks me so much that I well up. The picture shows a blonde, blue-eyed girl of around four, holding a faded-brown stuffed dog with long ears. It's Big-Dog, the teddy my daughter has slept with and carried around with her almost since the day she was born. I look at the headline: *They are 'civilised' and 'look like us': the racist coverage of Ukraine.* In the article, Moustafa Bayoumi asks, 'Are Ukrainians more deserving of sympathy than Afghans and Iraqis?' He offers evidence of what he considers to be warped media coverage, quoting a reporter in The Daily Telegraph who wrote, 'They seem so like us. That is what makes it so shocking. Ukraine is a European country. Its people watch Netflix and have Instagram accounts'. An Al Jazeera host says 'Looking at them, the way they are dressed, these are prosperous … I'm loath to use the expression … middle-class people.' Is this why I'm crying? Because they watch box sets and their daughters have IKEA stuffed toys? This is the first time an image from the war has affected me so strongly; I care more because this little girl looks like my own.

As the summer arrives, we move from *Paddington* to *Frozen*. Afterwards I show Molly the video of Amelia Anisovoych, the Ukrainian girl singing 'Let it Go' from her bomb-shelter at the start of the war. She wears a black jumper with white stars on it. She is seven years old and has gaps in her teeth. At the start of the video, filmed by a neighbour, babies are crying and people are shifting about and talking, but as she starts to sing the shelter falls silent. The video shows people lying on sleeping bags and sitting on folding chairs in a low-ceilinged basement. As she reaches the chorus, her voice rises and she closes her eyes.

Let it go, let it go
You'll never see me cry
Here I stand and here I stay
Let the storm rage on...

At Christmas I show Molly the West End actresses that played Anna and Elsa in the film joining Amelia as she sings at Wembley Arena. That December, as the sparkling trio perform on a London stage, the government halves the amount of money it gives councils for the settlement of Ukrainian refugees.

In May 2023, after more than a year of the Russo-Ukraine war, the blue and yellow ribbons outside Molly's nursery are taken down and replaced with red, blue and white bunting and Union Jacks. We are preparing for the coronation of the King. I take her to a party where the children wear gold cardboard crowns they have made themselves, adorned with jewels and stickers featuring the landmarks of London: Tower Bridge, Buckingham Palace, Big Ben. Like *Paddington*, Molly says. Let's watch that again.

During the Queen's Jubilee celebrations, Paddington had appeared with Her Majesty in a short film. They had tea together, shared a marmalade sandwich and he said, 'Thank you Ma'am. For everything.' When she died months later, people left pictures of the Queen and the bear walking hand in hand, and marmalade sandwiches, at memorial sites. As the national symbol of our kindness to refugees walked towards the pearly gates with our Queen, the first flight was scheduled to send people who had crossed the channel in small boats to Rwanda. This flight was prevented from taking off due to legal challenges but the government continues to push for it.

In June, Molly and I watch *Paddington* again. As the bear dances along to Tobago and D'Lime's calypso, the Home Office unit formed to prevent the recurrence of the 2018 Windrush scandal is being disbanded. As our country prepares to celebrate the seventy-fifth anniversary of the arrival of the Windrush vessel, Home Office minister Suella Braverman has decided it is time to 'move on'. After misclassifying hundreds of commonwealth-born people as illegal aliens – causing loss of employment, homes, passports and services, as well as wrongful detention and, in eighty-three cases, deportation

– the unit set up to fix the system is no longer needed, despite only 26% of claims for compensation having been awarded.

So now it is July, 2023. As I write this a new immigration law has just been passed to 'Stop the Boats'. We will no longer offer any asylum to people who have travelled here irregularly. The largest proportion of people crossing the Channel in small boats are now from Afghanistan, where thousands of British allies in the fight against ISIS and the Taliban were left abandoned and in grave danger. An Afghan pilot who fought with the British and recently arrived here on a small boat was threatened with deportation to Rwanda. In other boat news, amid local protests, we are moving five hundred young male asylum seekers onto the Bibby Stockholm, a barge docked off Portland Port in Dorset, where they will be housed in tiny bunk-bedded cabins with no right to work.

We bake cakes for a summer fair at the school to raise money for Ukrainian refugees, but I can't see many yellow and blue flags around the village anymore. Last night I looked up the origins of the Derbyshire flag. In my mind it was a banner that had been carried high in mediaeval processions and draped across the shoulders of victorious noblemen on horseback, and these were the stories I had relayed to Molly. The reality is somewhat more prosaic. In 2006 there was a competition led by BBC Radio Derby to design a flag after a listener called in to share how much he had enjoyed the displays of regional pride he witnessed when holidaying in Cornwall. The winning flag was blue and green; blue for the local rivers and green for the local countryside.

We fly our flags and we try to believe. But this insistence on Britain's virtue is a bit like the belief in Santa at a population level: I'll believe we are good for you, you believe we are good for me, and truth be damned. Perhaps then, there is a certain kind of beauty in the transparency of our Derbyshire flag's quotidian invention and the simplicity of what it celebrates. A lack of mythic historical grandeur, yes, but at least a story that's true.

POEMS
Dmytro Semchyshyn

### learning norwegian

i still haven't learned the word for war
but i know the word for home

don't know yet the verb to suffer
but i already can write 'i love you'

don't ask me what's the norwegian for scared
I can only say 'children', 'evening', 'happy'

how many new words
i still have to learn

2022

### The Phone Rang

The phone rang on and on
in a room
large like a minister's office
or that of the big boss[1] himself

the quivering r-r-r

---

[1] The original word *вождь* translates as leader, or chief. Older people in Ukraine still associate this word with totalitarian leaders such as Lenin and Stalin.

bounced off the table
the dusty rugs the armchair
floated down the hallway
the stairs
down

a large poster with a ruddy warrior
drawn with ink on paper
swayed on the wall

thrown from side to side,
the warrior almost got torn in half
but his hands held the gun
his white eyes looked at the window
the smile did not fade from his face

2017


**an exam**

*To Wislawa Szymborska*[2]

Answering the question what is Earth
City of God or a pest house
i fail the test
and feel like a student
who failed his parents' hopes

i look for the right answer but cannot find it
for i find that the right answer does not exist
and everything depends on the strength of one's own convictions
which grow boundless and turn into faith

---

[2] 'an exam' is inspired by 'The Two Apes of Brueghel' by the Polish poet, which deals with a difficult graduation exam.

and while i choose between those two
i think about another question in the exam
what is choice
if there is none it's bad
but when there is it's scary
and after prolonged reflection i understand
how much i am scared

and i come face to face with the test's third question
which utterly destroys all my hope
who am i

and i hear the whispered
prompts from those who have gone through their share of suffering
responses to the question i must answer all by myself

but i grow mute from anxiety and the thought
that i could give a wrong answer
and the test would go on forever

at the next table
an emperor is given a test by the god of war
he gets a failing grade

2017 [3]

### resurrection

i recall
how after an educational talk about the German settlements in our
    area
delivered by the head of the local German cultural centre
i saw a sombre man come up to him
he said that he had visited those areas and found something in the

---

[3] Although this year may seem to pre-date the Russian invasion, the current war in Ukraine began in 2014.

ground
and before leaving
he opened a bag and emptied its contents onto the table

i did not know the names of many things there so i had to guess
there were
bars with immobile wheels resembling fragments of clock
    mechanisms
flat parts of broken buckles
tiny circles with two openings inside them that were like broken
    buttons
a bent gilded flower with wide-open and sharp ends of petals that
    was similar to a lily

yet another thing was among those old bits and pieces
a metal figurine
its facial features eaten by corrosive wear
stumps of its thin arms raised up
a rusty nodule disfiguring its left leg
through its crossed-together feet a hole
there was no cross perhaps it stayed behind in the ground
or it rotted away or conversely was made of a more precious metal
and could therefore have been ripped off
leaving a deep hollow along its back

in the palm of my hand lay a tiny
figure of Christ
an aborted embryo
a tiny person who lived inside his mother's womb
but suffered corrosion
and was crucified
and then torn from the cross
and buried under a century-old layer of earth
together with deformed household items

the bible is an old book
the priests' words are but priests' words
the German settlers' interconfessional strife

is now remembered by none
and just like i didn't know the names of many things then
i still don't know them
but i know
that all of this happened again to us
and to me

something died and had to be reborn

But for resurrection still we wait

2017, 2022

Translated by Vitaly Chernetsky

**VÝBAČTE**
Casey Bailey

*after Dmytro Semchyshyn*

I still don't know how to ask for what I want
but I mastered *sorry* before

I let my head rest against the seat
of the plane. I will always stumble

through life, but will try to land on my own face
*Tut mir Leid, lo siento, désolé*

You can't plan your mistakes
but you can prepare for them

THE THIRTEENTH MONTH OF 2022
Bogdan Kolomiychuk

February 23, 2023
No, we will not remember only the frightening things, the terrible things. Funny things happen in this war too…

I'll never forget how I ran with a bucket of boiling water, naked to the waist, from the spot where I had warmed it, with all but my own soul, to the place where I intended to wash my head and do my laundry.

I could only think, 'Shit, if we get hit now... and I am here with this bucket of hot water... they'll say about me:

'He was running.'

'For his life?'

'No, to do his laundry...'

January 7, 2023
This year, for the first time, I feel like summing up the past year.

I've been meaning to do it right up until today, until I realised it's already January 7.

A whole week of the new year is gone, and I didn't even notice.

I don't feel like the previous year has ended yet. I can't let 2022 go. I will only let it go after we win. After the war. For now, it's the thirteenth month of 2022.

After we win, I hope I will know what to do with my experiences. With my Donbas inside me, with my memories and farewells.

And with everything unread and unwritten.

I hope we all do.

December 11, 2022
Today I helped the surgeons at the stabilisation centre. If a Book of Life is being kept somewhere out there, this page needs a bookmark.

## November 29, 2022

Yet another date when we were promised to be rotated out and sent to rest.

We don't believe the promises anymore. The date turned out to be a lie before.

We don't believe, but we still secretly hope.

We seem to talk about our previous, civilian lives more. Very cautiously, we share plans for the future. We listen to a hell of exhaustion spread through our bodies.

I miss silence. When there are no forays or hits. A morning quiet, when the city outside the window is still asleep, and the coffee-maker murmurs in the kitchen.

I miss so many things.

If I could live my life over again, I would make sure to enjoy every little thing.

Sometimes I whistle Slava Vakarchuk's song, 'When the day comes and the war ends.'

The war is not ending, but the dog from my previous station comes. 😊 He looks at me with his moist eyes at my feet.

'You'll take me to Lviv with you, won't you?' he seems to ask.

Maybe I will. He's a good dog. Good, but shameless.

## November 18, 2022

Today is the Armed Forces of Ukraine Sergeant's Day. My new (non-)professional holiday. I want to celebrate Writer's Day as a civilian in a peaceful Ukraine.

## November 14, 2022

Dawn in the burned-out villages seems like a strange accident. Why, you wonder, do the blackened skeletons of the houses need such vibrant sunlight? And still, it comes in sheaves, it fills the empty streets and the dead orchards, awakening in them one or two figures of the locals, who spend their nights hidden God knows where, and packs of abandoned dogs.

The dogs, even the biggest ones, are not aggressive. They come right up to us, nuzzle us, look into our eyes, beg for food. We share what we have with them and then for a long time cannot get rid of their company.

Beyond the ghost villages lie ghost pine-forests, cut through with black-and-grey potholed roads. Our trailer-truck hit a mine a few days ago, and now lies still, leaning onto its crippled right side. Our driver is visibly nervous when we go past it, and does everything to keep to the safe middle of the road. Further on, almost at the edge of the city, I recognise a railroad crossing and a station sign, pockmarked with shell fragments.

The city is coping better. The ruins here are sharper, but life is also more stubborn. Right in the street, you could trade cigarettes for milk and sheep-cheese from the farm-women astride old rusty bicycles. They say, the first cash-machine is working, and a branch of 'Nova Poshta'[1] will open up soon. Finally, mad with happiness, we find a small grocery store, charged with the smell of salted fish and the first one we've seen in forever...

Happiness, damn it, is in painfully simple things and joys.

Remind me of this, if I ever forget.

But I won't forget.

## November 7, 2022

Slashed trees, burned machinery, ruined houses. Sometimes I am surprised when my eye finds something solid and unharmed.

Such is my present reality.

My greatest consolation is cell phone service which one gets here and there.

And music, music, music. Loaded up, prudently, ahead of time, in better times. Chopin, Debussy, Elgar, Silvestrov, Holst, Satie...

No explosions can overcome it. This music is louder than artillery shells, even when it's playing softly and delicately in my earphones.

## October 22, 2022

First hours of leave – the square in front of the railway station, where the military give each other – strangers all – a friendly greeting. This kind of incomparable fraternal spirit.

The little girl, who reminded me of my daughter, asked to hug me.

Hoards of beggars and the disgusting (but so good!) railway station coffee.

---

[1] Literally 'New Post', a courier service.

The empty compartment.

The Ukrainian Railways burgers which I consume like Gargantua, making the waitress think they don't feed us in the army.

The poems from the 1920s which I've come to love during my time in service.

Dreams and plans...

The most beautiful views outside my window.

The soothing metronome of the carriage's wheels.

Road-drowsiness.

And all of it is mine.

## October 16, 2022

Cold nights, bright dawns, and silver on the grass. First frost on the steppe.

We've been issued warm fleece jumpers *à la* Zaluzhnyi. Mine is a size too small.

But it's no matter, I'll stretch it.

Knowing the kindness of my friends, let me ask right away, please don't offer to send me the right one. I have another one.

For now, I am making coffee with my fingers, numb with cold, and breathing the fresh, crystal-clear air. And thanking you, Lord, for one more morning.

## October 2, 2022

Sometimes I put on my civilian clothes instead of the uniform. Today, I found my Covid mask in my pocket. What nostalgia this brought on!

Say what you will, those were the good times! 😀

## September 23, 2022

September rains water the steppe generously. Moisture gets under your clothes, into your backpack; it rusts your weapon. My friend who is keeping a hand-written journal had to dry out the soaked pages, which made the writing on them look like ancient Sanskrit.

Every now and then, someone emerges from the watery sieve and walks up to you, asking, 'Do you have any coffee?'

'I do. Sit down...'

'It's the real stuff! Thank God!' they say, with so much joy in their tired, hoarse voices, as if this were not coffee but a handful of gold dust.

We run from one warm place to the next. Our temporary home is wherever our boots are drying.

One writes well in the rain. Or used to... Stories plotted earlier ripen and bother you like an aching tooth. When they hurt especially badly, I put on the rain slicker and wander in the abandoned orchard. 'Lemberg, Vienna, Poznan, Berlin, 1905, 1910, 1914... especially 1914.'

I wander, like a ghost, until I get tired. Then I leave the orchard but everything I haven't written follows behind me. Like a sad, rain-soaked dog.

## September 15, 2022

There are three things you can watch endlessly: a fire burning, water running, and our troops coming in with captured enemy machinery. 😳 😳 Good morning!

## September 5, 2022

I emerge from a night shift with a feeling of pathos.

When we come back from the war, we will be the greatest generation in our history. We will write the greatest novels and the best music. We will give the greatest performances in film and on stage. We will be the best doctors and scientists. The best lovers, husbands, and wives. We will be the soul of every party, and also philosophers and bores who mutter to themselves...

We will be like that because our generation is the one that will break the vicious circle of Ukrainian history that trapped all our ancestors.

We will change our state and we will change Europe.

We will be like that because we have learned to cherish life in all its manifestations, in its shortest moments.

Because we will never accept another Ukraine. Only the one we are fighting for.

## September 2, 2022

As the cold weather approaches, the local mice attempt to establish contact with us. They scurry, sometimes, right next to our boots. They hide behind our backpacks, run in twos and threes from one corner to another. And all you hear is: 'Psst, soldier... Glory to Ukraine! Putin *khuylo*... Got any food?'

August 31, 2022

For the first time, I won't be with my daughter for September 1st. But I know the people behind whose backs our children will start the new school year tomorrow. The hooligans who told stories today of the shenanigans they pulled off when they were at school.

Theirs are the most loyal backs.

And it's also autumn tomorrow. It's finally here.

August 30, 2022

I've been promoted to Junior Sergeant. My rise in the military is steeper than in literature... 😂😂

August 23, 2022

Do not touch my laundered fatigues and shined boots! Those are for Independence Day...

You'd think it was Christmas, seriously.

Come on, just a little bit longer.

August 20, 2022

Scorching days in our steppe are slowly giving way to cool weather. You feel it especially at night, when you have to wrap yourself in warm clothes. You end up wrapping your weapon as well, and it nuzzles you like a trusting cat.

We breathe in the thick night air, inhale it greedily, as if we'd grown an extra pair of lungs. Steeped with steppe grasses and the first scents of autumn, it is delicious and even a touch intoxicating, like new wine. Someone lights up a cigarette and sends a silver thread of smoke through the darkness.

'It's cold, damn it,' you hear them say. 'I wonder what it's like in Lviv?'

I shrug, although I'm probably not the one being asked.

What is it like... I used to look forward to this, my favourite season, every year. With all its urban problems, utilities failures, and long rains. Pouting, like the ticket lady at the commuter rail station, but also familiar. You don't choose your favourite season, just as you don't choose any of the things you love most.

Let it come then.

There, and here.

## August 13, 2022

Yesterday, I finally made it out to the village to go to the hairdresser's. She is a former teacher who knows how to cut hair and now tidies the soldiers' heads.

When I asked her to trim my beard, she looked at me as if I had proposed something indecent.

'No, young man! You can do that yourself.'

And then she watched, silently and from a distance, as I groomed my beard which during my service here had come to resemble a thorn bush.

And in the entire last month, there was nothing nicer than the touch of the three-millimetre clipper-head on my face.

And no better sound than the buzz of the worn-out clippers.

It'll grow back, I thought, and I'll come again. To my new barbershop. 😳

## August 8, 2022

Good Lord, the melons here!

Small, tight and sweet (yes, I am talking about melons).

When you hold a slice of this bliss, it warms your hands like a piece of the sun itself.

And when the alarm sounds, the choice is very real: run to cover or finish eating this ambrosia.

Take the melon and run, you would say.

And you would be right. 😳

## August 5, 2022

The new conditions give rise to new, sometimes odd urges and desires.

For instance, I am dying to put on a freshly laundered starched shirt.

(Right, with my fatigue trousers and uniform jacket. 😳 I'd be a sight.)

Or, I have decided I will get a cat after the war.

(Come on now. Me and a cat? Only one of us will survive.)

And today I put milk into my tea.

(Which I had previously considered a form of culinary perversion.)

In short, I'm beginning to be afraid of myself.

Because we are changing these steppes, and the steppes are changing us.

August 3, 2022

When I was a kid, I used to love toy aeroplanes and dreamed of seeing a fighter-plane up close.

I really, really wanted to see it.

Dear universe, can you please stop fulfilling my childhood dream? 😳 Or at least, do it less often, or less loudly? I'm all grown up now.

August 1, 2022

I have refused all interview requests since February 24.

At first, when I just got mobilised, it felt like the talking should be done by those who are at the front. Now, when I'm far away from home too, I'm convinced that we should listen to the people who've been fighting the longest.

Finally, I agreed to an interview – and stumbled.

I wanted to tell the interviewer that things are often funny here, despite the pain. We joke a lot, and our jokes have become sharp and slightly cynical.

We miss our homes, but also create a temporary home for ourselves.

We cherish things that used to be everyday: fresh bread, real coffee, a hot dinner, clean clothes, a chance to call home.

That's what I wanted to say – but for some reason I couldn't. I botched the interview.

Just like I still don't have anything intelligent to say on the topic of 'A Writer in the Army' or 'Literature During the Time of War' or 'What the World is Going to Look Like Afterwards'. I don't know. Honestly, I don't know. And I can't even imagine it.

Maybe I do not speak now so that I'll be able to speak when I come back. I'll go on and on then! Just try to stop me.

July 29, 2022

We miss books desperately, even though we wouldn't have a lot of time to read them. I could find no room in my backpack for my trusted Kindle. Now I regret it.

I'd cherish a good book more than a pair of rubber sandals. And those – trust me – are a real asset 😳 (my brothers-in-arms won't let me lie). I've lost and found mine twice already.

Today I pictured myself finding an abandoned library and

running my finger across the spines of the books on the shelf, one dusty title to the next. Until I finally find something that can fill the space left vacant in my backpack. I was able to imagine all this very clearly, like a movie. It must be the heat here.

## July 26, 2022
At night, giant bejewelled stars shine above the steppe. I've never seen anything like them.

In the daytime, tiny obnoxious gnats fly above the steppe and drive you crazy.

As you have probably guessed, I like the stars more than the gnats.

## 24 July 2022
Today, I washed in a river whose name I don't know.

It was my first bath in several days. And the first one so close to the enemy. I will probably remember for the rest of my life the touch of the muddy green water on my body, the smell of the grasses on the banks, the wind, and the river mud.

A little bit of the steppe will forever stay under my skin. And these winds – in my lungs.

## June 19, 2022
Let us be civilian dads next year. Let us hug our children every day, living in our peaceful cities and villages. In a Ukraine that borders a no-man's land that was once called 'rf'.[2] Happy Fathers' Day to everyone involved!

## June 18, 2022
I saw the way two soldiers wearing the same armoured vest sized each other up.

Forget about women who put on the same dress. 😳

## April 13, 2022
My mind tends to associate particularly memorable books or stories with specific intervals of time. For instance, I remember that I read Backman's *A Man Called Ove* last winter, in January. I read Barnes

---

[2] Russian Federation.

in summer. And now I associate the war with Robert Musil's expansive and multifaceted prose.

With the 'tactical' Kindle in the pocket of my uniform.

With waiting for good news.

With love despite the hate.

### March 15, 2022

Before the start of the war, our literary community was clamouring for a native Hemingway. Now he is certain to appear.

### February 28, 2022

First twenty-four hours spent entirely in my unit. I check the internet. See a site with my books.

It's like that wasn't me. Like I'm not an author. A different life.

### February 25, 2022

At the recruitment office: 'By the time you sort us out, the war will be over! Get a move on!'

'There are so many of you! There won't be enough Russians!'

Translated by Nina Murray

## MAY YOU HAVE MOUNTAINS OF MELONS
Niall Griffiths

And in February 2022 I was chiding myself for not doing Dry January. I was trying to write a haiku about my Christmas belly that would have 18 syllables to reflect a sense of flabbiness. And I've often thought: why would you choose the darkest, most miserable time of the year to forego alcohol? A time of post-festivities, of brief grey days, is not optimal to resist the temptations of liquid sunshine. You can choose when to detox and when to intox. Look at the sky for the signs.

And you, Bogdan? You were looking upwards for different things. You were on the lookout for shrieking steel and flame. Machines of massive malice. You were living in a ditch, a trench, and knowing your earth in a way that invaders do not know and will never know and have never known.

You say you can't let go of '22. Only when you win will you be able to do that, and until then you will calibrate your calendar with something like 'AP': After Putin, perhaps. Year zero. And may we all live AP; may you help us to all live AP. You carry your Donbas inside you and, really, the epoch of AP began there, in 2014, didn't it? Or maybe even in Abkhazia in 2008. Or in Grozny in the late 90s, when the lone child with total hell in his eyes crept out from the ruins and found an undamaged tricycle to pedal through the smoking wreckage and around the corpses and body parts (the eyewitness description is seared into my psyche). Maybe then. Or maybe in the extravagant sportswash of the World Cup and the red carpets laid out in London for vory oligarchs, the red better to disguise the blood squelching out of their shoes. Yes, maybe then: AP year 1.

In Tbilisi recently, amongst the anti-Russian graffiti, I was drawn to one item: a Georgian flag alongside a diminutive caricature of the

Russian presidential psychopath. This piece was entitled 'LILIPUTIN'. A fine example of Swiftian wordplay. The world needs protection from inadequate little men; there is no more dangerous a creature on the face of the planet than a man who is terrified of being seen as a wimp. Dig, Bogdan; the berms you build girdle the globe.

This journal is your truth, Bogdan, and this is THE truth; a concept become alien now. Objective reality is a notion to be debated, a mutable idea, but not for you; you see and recognise and know lies. Even as 'the hell of exhaustion' spreads through you, you hold to the truth as you hold to your earth. We are not all living in the Russkiy Mir and the very episteme is shell-shocked. You allow yourself to envisage a futurity. You miss silence; you miss so many things. Humanity itself misses, yearns for, the very things that you are fighting to reinstate, to protect the remnants of, and so build upon; this is what any tomorrow must have as a foundation. And the beauties that tremble on the very edge of destruction – such stuff is known to you, Bogdan. You love the 'good, shameless' dog. I hope you will live with him in Lviv in a time to come. Such is what the future could be.

Ghost villages, ghost forests. So many ghosts. The 'mad happiness' occasioned by the first salted fish you've seen 'in forever'. How the joys shrink in a world made infernal; 'remind us of this, if we ever forget'. Yes, Bogdan, we'll return the favour. Physically small, psychologically immense – a favourite food, hot tea; hold such tiny things against the colossal megalomania that eagerly creates an ocean of blood. A millennium of pain. Hold these things against the rotting cadaver of Ilyin, hissing in Putin's ear; Rus must be great. Eternal war. Only Rus defends civilisation from barbarism. Prove this through massacre of the innocents.

Kyiv Rus, founded by those who established the city on the banks of the Dnipro; the word 'Rus' from an old Scandi language, meaning 'those who row'. The original founders weren't Slavic. This is a truth, but the saviour of Rus must come from beyond historical fact; and that is myth, and in warped minds, myth wins. But you, Bogdan, your 'present reality' is death and destruction. Carnage put upon you. And music, always music, which 'no explosions can overcome'. Also a truth. Small and gigantic joys.

You reference Rabelais, Debussy, Chopin. You are fond of smiley emojis. You thank your God for each morning. Your humour always rises: the comparative good old days of the Covid pandemic. Your truth, Bogdan. THE truth.

And the gems of your words: 'there are three things you can watch endlessly: a fire burning, water running, our troops coming in with captured enemy machinery'. Your smiley emojis are diamonds. And your future shines like the perfect city just over the horizon; how you will rebuild from these ashes. How you will honour the miracles of your existence; how you will be the best human beings it is possible to be. Such will be the greatest victory over the shrivelled souls in the Kremlin. It will be the ultimate triumph.

'Like a trusting cat' does your gun nuzzle you and that night, in bed, storm outside, as I hold my purring tomcat, hypnagogia turns him into the weapon that I must nurture and keep clean and functional because my life, and the lives of others, depend entirely on that.

May you have a mountain of melons, Bogdan. May you get your cat, and your dog, and your place in Lviv. And may you never be afraid of yourself, however such self-analysis stands as a beautiful corrective to the cowardice of your enemy. They decided to stand in violent opposition to you; such a dichotomy did not grow from the soil. This was their choice.

And God, Bogdan, how you can write: your entry for August 3rd, 2022 says more about the sheer oddness of the human condition than many novelists manage in 400 pages. Sow these words.

'Things are funny here, despite the pain': let this be mankind's epitaph.

I'm reading your journal alongside Babel's *1920 Diary* and Snyder's *Road to Unfreedom*. If I used the cliché that obviously offers itself here, I'd do a disservice to the power of the words of all three of you, but it does stand true – it stands infuriatingly, horribly, despairing true. We learn nothing. If there's one constant in the human story it's that we learn nothing, notwithstanding the plenitude of lessons. And also that we forever yearn for some kind of inner peace, some stilling of the turmoil inside us, and we'll gleefully indulge in endless violence in an attempt to attain such calm.

The little mice, Bogdan. They approach you for warmth. They

'flicker, sometimes, right next to our boots'. When humanity is at its worst, it is also at its best. And against Bucha, Irpin, Mariupol, there is you, Bogdan, observing the tiny animals.

The image of the two soldiers in the same armoured vests regarding each other resentfully like two women wearing the same dress at a party. Insert smiley emoji.

I read and re-read your words, Bogdan. As I write, I can see, through my window, the ruby berries on my rowan tree; guardian against evil spirits, supposedly, in the myth-kitty of my land. A male blackbird sits on a branch. I'll send you his song, Bogdan. My greatest hope is that I, we, the world, will be gifted with more of your words. That you'll be allowed to sing more. And in return – and I know it's not enough, but it's all we have – we'll send you weapons, and corn, and sunflowers, which were already yours anyway. The golden wheat-fields and cloudless blue skies of your flag. Love and luck and gratitude to you.

## Distant Bird V Formations
Rostyslav Melnykiv

      ringing silence
                               will grow bitter at the bottom
      autumn will draw
                       cities in maps
      outside the window
             *a pilgrim will flash by*
      the soothsayer will convey
                   who has
                          turned
                               into him
Back in the day
    You
caught
   a Bird
Grandpa called it
   the Sun
  and set it free . . .
But
no one knew
        that
   *shards*
   *of a broken mirror –*
       that is all
   that remained
           of
             the land
      of wandering seminarians
           Silence the Mystery Play,

oh Formel:
the Steppe has been wasted . . .
Somewhere
*on the map of Eurasia*
August fades
wondrous Scythians move
Westward
in their carts
And heavenly paths wither like haulm

Everything passes . . .
our melancholy knights
are Dreamt of by Dragons
their brain hemispheres turned Autumnal
and the Gods' night watch
like a Wheel
off its Axle
Knocks off the Galaxy's Departure Timetable

This is what the Trumpets lamented, what the Hunt wrapped up
a Generation, an Era, or what do you call it
And
on the points
of eye pupils
falls
in a twist
T H E  U N I V E R S E
Oh my
Goddess
the very last
Mare's
head[1]

My
God

---

[1] Mare's Head (*kobyliacha holova*) is a character from Ukrainian folktales. This image is also extensively played with in Volodymyr Rafeyenko's recent novel *Mondegreen* (available in English translation from Harvard UP).

                    Let's start
                    this Journey
                    at High Noon
     so that at the sun's Zenith someone would steal the rooster from the spire
                and someone would recite the Quran from the Minaret
                  when we set out Westward, but not for commerce


                    but for War – let it be so: Allah is Great
                    Sabres are sharpened. Messengers blow their horns
                    My God is this path glorious or deadly
                    Forty days long and one foot wide


                              But
                         It's time to go
                     – the clock strikes on the tower
              – the captives and the wives already have their own wailers
                              and
                            the rain
                          is all speech:
                       H E L V E T I U S
                              AND
                            *a day*
                        *that's like a lance*
                           that you
                            oh Lord
                        hold in thy hands


This is *the final prayer*
                    God has long disappeared
The cosmos collapsed behind the door
                    and it's as if I never existed
We leave this country
                    with the last waves of the Gauls
Leave it to ashes
                    like Lot once did
Not romantic temptations
                    extinguished fires of autumnal sun
Actually, all is topsy-turvy

                              – the rest the soothsayer can tell you
We set out on a campaign
                    glorious non-Zaporozhian knights [2]
Tumble down a field going there
                    and tumble right back in the other direction.

These vanishing spaces:
                    not shameful, not hard to capture
Not like killing a dragon
                    that's stuck in your brain like the steppe
The sounds of the final prayer
                    every time we err
And the final steps
                         those
                                brought over
                                    by
                                         echo

he is now gone . . .
                    he is now gone . . .
the wheels rattle the funeral march . . .
                         harmonicas play,
                              weed is being smoked . . .
westward . . .
          westward . . .
                    westward . . .
one train car after another . . .
          one after another . . .
                    soldiers fill those cars . . .
marching companies,
          storming battalions
khaki-coloured hum
          fills the train cars
westward . . .
          westward . . .

---

[2] The poem alludes to the traditional sixteenth-seventeenth century formula referring to Zaporozhian Cossacks as 'glorious knights'.

                         westward . . .
    but he
            is not
                     among them . . .
                         he is
                                   now
                                          gone . . .
too thin is *the web of life*
one train car after another,
                     one after another . . .
. . .
blood flows down the ground . . .
blood thickens in the sky . . .
                              the sun is setting . . .
echelons are moving westward . . .
                       echelons
                                    are
                                          moving
                                                    westward
   a sun ray fades on a bayonet's blade,
      the guard adjusts his machine gun . . .
but
    he is
         now
             gone . . .


                                    *my republic's trains*
                          don't always arrive on time
                               my republic's trains
                     don't always know their next station
                 sometimes they wander off and never return
                        a desperate scream pierces the railway
                                             they say
                 this is the ghost of the first steam locomotive wailing
                        its tracks burned through this wiry steppe
                                     my republic's trains
                          never pay attention to such trifles

                their wheels always rattle off new rhythms for old legends
                and this gives reason not to pay attention to such trifles
                      even if the rails go rusty and the ties rot away
                    even if all the semaphores and lights are switched off
                        even if the network maps yellowed with time
                              do not foresee any movement
                      and all the tracks lead to a dead end
                                  my republic's trains
                                  slice through silence
                                      they keep going
                                              for
                                            they
                                  just like my republic
                                  do not have a choice

and you won't count the sea waves wastefully, one after the other,
        as the wind fills the sails and the oars are raised high . . .
where is that God-promised island
                for surprise,
                          for a feat,
                                    for a breath? –
space is captured by mind,
              and in the sky fade away
                        *the distant bird v formations . . .*

                                  Translated by Vitaly Chernetsky

HACKLE
R. M. Francis


Shadowed pilgrim remapping strange conurbations
of autumnal hemispheres, becomes a soothsayer
within vanishing spaces, where birds flock in Vs
above the steppe: vagabundi of far-off peace.

The news breeds
like tuber stems of spuds and beans
and we sit too close – eyes blinkered from God
in the twist of 24hr rolling screens
and the sham icons of digital scenes – to see.

Formel soars in the last thermals of Kyiv,
tastes set on the chalk-dusting of Zhilianska Street,
where sunflower murals peak through collapse.
Its call calls the few back to Job, Isaiah, Hosea.

One dropped feather amongst the wreckage of war
whispers for us if we care to reckon.

## The Grey Coat of Silt
Ivan Andrusiak

⋆. ⋆. ⋆

when the moon hangs still above the lake
and artillery rests
for even artillery sometimes needs
to cool its barrels
then a black god comes out of the lake
and like a lunatic
wanders its shores

he gathers the craters of bombs
shells and mines
into a large transparent sack
packs them tightly

'need to go deeper –'
he mumbles to himself
'need to go deeper'

and when the dawn comes
and the artillery wakes for its morning workout
the black god throws
the enormous sack packed with craters
as big as half the world
over his shoulder
and smoothly
unhurriedly
dives into the black stillness

'need to go deeper –'
the sound bubbles up
'need to go deeper'


*. *. *


winters aren't in the business of convincing
they just rip off the slender skin of snow
under the icon-like dense canopy of trees

this is the place of sleep – and here, pressing bosoms
to the great root, a multitude keeps warm
the plants you do not dare search for
they cannot open up before spring comes

but an uncertain bullet might arrive
from heights that are unbearably dark
and smash its tin eye flat against the night

only then some plants might wake for a moment
some would burn out in the midst of snow
and some too might fully wither


*. *. *


only in some places now the lake is frozen
but water can be seen
in unsubdued transparency
so prickly and thick
as if the tiny sparkles of ice
are hesitating

and only when through the thick clouds
a golden ray is able to break through
then the soul of frozen water
down deep

will keep warm warm warm
in the grey coat of silt
everyone whom the Lord has chosen
straight from the heart
straight from the heart

\*. \*. \*

the fish looked into the water's eye
come – it said – come and wash away
the muddy traces
of winter

the eye did not blink
only vessels somewhere in the depths
strained
and cracked

November-December 2022
Vytivka-Berezan'

Translated by Vitaly Chernetsky

IN GREY COUNTRIES NOT SO FAR FROM HERE
Anthony Cartwright

I

In November the people would fall with the leaves and drop right there on the pavement. They lay dead all day. Days sometimes, although never too long, because of the dogs that came now to roam the towns with the rising smell of the bodies carried on the autumn winds. Evenings, the handsome street sweeper would come to sweep the bodies up, as if for a bonfire, and ward off the dogs with his broom. Then he would sing the bodies back to life.

And life would return with his song through the winter months, with strings of lights between the busy market stalls and the people going about their business, buying bread and cheese and barrels of beer and stamping their feet around the brazier fires and forgetting they had ever died. Until those bitterest weeks in February when the coal would always run low and the people would die again and lie frozen on the hard ground.

Come the thaw, come the street sweeper, singing his songs of life, and he would plant the bodies in the mud at the edge of town and wait for them to sprout in the spring and grow back to life again.

The summer would warm them. May and June were the easiest months with the fairs and the wakes weeks and the long blue nights of revelry before the fiercest heat came with the southern winds and the people burned slowly and turned to ash.

That's when the street sweeper would come, in his broad brimmed hat, and sweep the dust and shape it into new people and they would rise again in cool September and live sober and undramatic lives until they fell once more with the November winds.

And so went the years and the people were happy, with only the small, nagging doubt that the handsome street sweeper became more bent, his voice more cracked, and his handsome face more lined with his efforts and that there might, perhaps, be no one to one day replace him.

## II

When the days shortened the dog tide would come. The girl remembered that was what they always used to call it. She remembered little else, tried not to remember.

She lived on her own in a ruined cottage on a slope below where the woods had grown through the old works, above the stream and the empty canal, with a vegetable patch out by the front door and a view up to the town and the castle on the hill, but no road going past.

When the winds came and the leaves began to pattern the banks she would see strange birds and smoke rise from the town and the smell of it would mix with that of the fallen leaves and the dogs would come from the woods. You would hear them howling first and then they would come padding by. In small packs on the first morning, yelping at each other and chasing their tails and the drifting leaves. Then with more purpose and greater numbers. A surging wave of them.

The girl would move up the rickety stairs to what had been her bedroom once upon a time. The ceiling had collapsed and opened to the sagging roof. There were holes where you could watch the clouds scudding by and the odd bird come from the castle flapping its wings against the wind. She would put buckets and bowls down to try to catch the rain.

The dogs would leap now up the cottage windows and doors, slavering, with a gleam in their eyes and their ribs showing through their patchy, motley fur. The dogs poured from the works and the darker woods beyond, around the cottage like water round a river boulder, a river of fur and teeth and hungry bellies rising beneath the girl's window. She was hungry too, almost all of the time.

When the back door gave way to the sound of panting and the skittering of paws on floorboards she clambered through one of the holes to sit there on the uneasy roof tiles, clinging to the chimney pot and hoping it would end soon.

Away above the castle, the smoke drifted into the clouds and the birds flapped this way and that in the wind. The girl heard the scrabble and tumble of dogs against the bedroom door and clung tighter to the chimney pot. She thought that perhaps her time had come, as she had thought so many times since she had lived here on her own, and watched as the dogs massed as one, through the meadow and across the stream at the wide, shallow point where it curved and then up the line of the old canal towards the town.

On the wind she heard the sound of flapping, like that of a groundsheet snagged on a nail against a wall, craned her neck to see one of the castle birds come close, closer than she'd ever seen one. It was then that she saw that it wasn't a bird, but an umbrella, turning furiously inside and out, a few broken spokes glinting in the low sun, and riding on the wind. It settled on the roof beside her. The dogs were in the room below now, leaping and snapping through the gaps in the tiles at where she sat.

More flapping, bat-like wings of another umbrella, bigger this one, like the ones the fishermen used to use in the days when they'd come to sit between the stream and the canal, flasks of tea and sandwiches with them, sports commentary playing softly on little radios by their side. None of these for years now. And then another umbrella. A whole flock of these strange umbrella birds moving on the wind and alighting now on the cottage roof all around her. Mostly grey and black, but the odd small splash of colour within, and a pink one with a flamingo head for its handle just below her feet in the mossy guttering. A dog's head came through a hole in the roof and a few of the umbrellas scattered. She saw the dog's yellow teeth, as its gleaming eyes caught hers and then felt herself lifting, falling she thought, no – lifted! – raised up into the air, with the handles of a score of umbrellas under her ankles and knees and shoulders.

Up she went, above the dog tide and the dog, now howling, with its head and shoulders through the hole next to where she had sat. Up above the empty canal, with the skeletons of the old works buildings still visible through the trees and the older woods beyond. And as she rose towards the height of the town, she saw the lock gates that went all the way up the hill like steps for giants and the patchwork of houses and fields and factories below, black and green and black and green, and the bone-coloured castle up above on the hill top, with the streets winding themselves around it, with the fierce flapping of the umbrella wings in her ears as she was borne away on the wind.

III

In a field a man lay sleeping. He lay very still on his back, with a broom and iron pan leaning against a little rubbish cart next to him, as if a knight at rest, with a lance and shield and an armour-clad horse waiting for him to wake.

The girl thought the man was dead as she approached, set down in the field by the umbrella birds who flew away now in a winding spiral back over the ridge where the girl assumed the town to be. The wind dropped, and the silence rushed into her ears, no flapping wings, no hungry dogs, just the breeze in the hedgerow and a few bird calls and this dead man lying on the grass.

Then the man stirred and blinked and his eyes went wide at the sight of the girl. She saw now how very old he was, in his ruined boots and his torn overalls, his eyes bright in his creased face.

'So, you've come at last,' is what he said and sat up and motioned for the girl to sit beside him. and she hesitated for a moment until he reached for his bag that hung from his rubbish cart and took out some sandwiches and two neat slices of cake and apples and a flask with two cups and laid these out to share.

So they sat there in the field, with the town there beyond the ridge, invisible, but for the smudge of drifting smoke becoming cloud above the hill. The man talked as they ate and motioned in the direction of the town. He said that he was glad she was here and that there was much work to do and songs to learn, but that they had time, and they would get it all done in the end.

**BLOODIED EARTH**
**Liudmyla Taran**

Where will we go?
In our bodies
We feel
Our daughters and sons
Torn from life
Grass won't grow over them
Blood will flow from them
In a slow trickle
Day and night
For thousands of years we've nurtured this earth
For thousands of years we've raised beautiful children
For You Dear Lord
Yours is the vengeance
My torn words blown away by the wind
They fall into the cratered earth
That brims with blood

★★★

The broken ribs of our suffering
Basements, hideouts, shelters
For hope and despair
Pull them from under the rubble
Risen from ashes
Wash them with the water of life
Breathe their soul back into them
As our Lord once did
Miracles happen
We look at you with our empty eye sockets
Do not forgive murderers

★★★

The earth gapes
Blood runs
From the explosion
No time
Life's been
Scattered to pieces
Shot through the eye of a newborn

To curl into a poppy seed
To flee
To the ends of the world
There's no more world
Only the shadow and fire and what has been burned
And the newborn
Who could save
God

★★★

The child grown old with terror
Gone grey to the bones
Of your body raped by fear
How will you grow
How will you carry
This iron-stuffed earth
On your fragile war
Bones

★★★

Wheels of sand and clay
We are refugees
We carry
Cool immobile shadows
Of our homes on our shoulders
The ruins and exit wounds

That will never close
The wheels of sand
And raw clay carry us
To the land of numb forgetting

★★★

Everything she had saved for her death
She'd given away
For the victory
Down to the last penny
Left nothing for herself
*I want to live long enough to see it*

She reminds me sometimes
Of that one portrait
The vest and the wrinkles, the eyes
Pierced with pain as if with a blade
And the news that bursts
From the very heart of the earth

★★★

Sometimes you catch yourself thinking:
It's good that our dead who passed
Before the war
Know nothing of it.
Or else they would die all over again,
Crucified with the pain and the fear.
So many deaths already,
Piled all the way to the sky.
Hearts burned out
Down to black, black blood.
Or perhaps it is our dead
Who are pulling up this sky above us –
Otherwise the bloody earth
Would have fallen
Into the abyss.

\*\*\*

Wash the knives, beat the earth clean
Of the blood and the hatred. Where,
Where did their wings,
detached from their golden bodies,
fly to?

In my heart – arrows, bullets, and fire.
And the steppe
              frozen
                          vertically.
And death survived from the land of Cain,
spawned
      a hideous monster.

Days are hard as if forged from screams.
Nights are crumpled like paper.
Who engendered this serpent's race
that have forgotten God's wrath and vengeance?

                                  Translated by Nina Murray

BLOODIED EARTH
Kerry Hadley-Pryce


Imagine this: later on, I'll step outside. You will come with me. It is a kind of monsoon season here in the Black Country. Sometimes the heat sends shimmers across the tarmacked roads. Sometimes hail falls, yes, like bullets on the roof. Sometimes breath is vapour, or sweat is. But night has crumpled like paper, and I will step outside, and you will come with me. And you and I will feel everything that has ever happened because it is impossible to take more than three steps without encountering ghosts round here. Here, we all move within this enclosed landscape whose landmarks constantly draw us towards the past. Something about the shifting of the angles, the receding of the perspectives, the way the underground mines make the earth move, the soil. You and I will look at the lie of the land, the architecture. We will walk down the High Street. Imagine it, the particular hypnotic effect of the dissonance of it here. Here, there are districts corresponding to a whole spectrum of diverse feelings: the bizarre quarter, the happy quarter, the useful quarter, the safe quarter. We will drift through it, you and I. You'll see it, you'll hear it. Listen. Let yourself feel it.

Imagine this: you and I, just walking, together. Perhaps the day will be losing light by then. Perhaps there will be an early day moon. Our stepping will be the same, only a fine thread between us. We won't speak, but we'll know what each other is thinking. We'll look at buildings within which there are rooms more conducive to dreams than any drug. We'll lean against the railings of the subway, because we can do that. Men will pass by – young men, let's say, wearing beanie hats and checked shirts and skinny jeans and pointy shoes – checking their phones. Mothers pushing their children in strollers will pass us. They'll smile, at us, at you and I. And you and I will smile back. We'll see the crowds in cafés drinking coffee out of tall glasses. We'll hear music coming from behind large, black doors.

'Come,' I'll say. And we will walk out across the town, past the shop where the women laugh and the smell of fruit is thick and strong, like some kind of perfect summer. It's not far to the green borderlands, the long strip of the canal. And there, that place will be dead calm, and I will say – I will point out – the rise and fall of the land there, the life in it, the potential, like the soft spot of a baby's head. And there will come a distinct smoothing of the air, a ripeness of breeze that will rattle the trees. You will notice the lazy grumbling of pigeons, the frozen hurry of the horses. You will look at the bridge, and the wild plants growing out of the bricks there, and I will say something about porous boundaries and think I'm so clever, so safe to be clever here, and I'll wonder if you understand. And through, and on, come on, imagine this: there will be nettles, and we, you and I, will see them and though we will not touch them, we'll imagine the feel of the complexion of their leaves, the audacity of the prickle of their sting. And perhaps we'll see the heron, more dinosaur than bird, its precise and ardent focus trained on something in the water that we cannot, and will not ever, see.

'Come,' I'll say, and you will notice the colour of the earth, red, and you will think of bloodied earth, but this is our Black Country with its memories of days that were hard and mines that were deep. And look, imagine this: there will be men with tattooed arms. Fishermen. Quiet men, smoking by the water's edge. They are a type, this kind of man. They are patient and still. They wait. I, and you, will wonder what they're thinking, exactly. And I will look at you then. I will look at your face, at the way you're experiencing this place, at the way you're processing the sensations of it.

'Come,' I'll say, and we will walk up into the woods where, when the sun shines, the dappled, slanting light will flicker, and you and I will look like a spell has been cast on us, or like we've walked through a phantom. And we will be like ships in a bottle there, you and I, our threads pulled, and we will billow in the still air there. We will feel it though, both of us, something far away: a quickening. And I will stop and listen for the sound of the sun there. You will hear it, too, the way that our senses buy into the synaesthesia of it all, that siren call of safety.

'Come,' I'll say – imagine my voice – and we will hurry across the field, our feet dampened by last night's rain, and out over the scrubland at the back of the industrial estate. Just as we pass the church, I will see your eyes flicker with a memory, or a thought. There are hawthorn trees along the border, yew trees, and a thread of spider's web will catch against your hair. I'll notice and you'll laugh as I try to take it.

But later, imagine this: I will drape that thread across my computer here, and I will watch as it dithers against the warmth and the words. Fragile, like us.

WHEN YOU GROW UP
Roksolana Zharkova


When You Grow Up

Autumn smooths out the wrinkles in God's name.
Fruit falls to the ground as if shot down by rockets.
    Listen, when you grow up
    (and I'll be with you when you grow up)
Tell me, child,
Will there be anyone who will love us, so rootless?
Who will love us, so rootless and so unblooming?
Who will want to set us free in a sky filled with combat?
Who will appoint us as guards of their altars?
    The screaming turns your lungs into a bunch of grapes
    That are stomped and turn words into wine
    collected in the urns that are our cities' courtyards.
Rain showers drench us in the Blessed Sacrament
A few spare loaves of bread are handed out
'Take a couple,' someone tells you,
'They've just been brought in from the bakery.'
You reach out your arms expecting
the miracle of five loaves of bread and two of your favourite candies
While someone puts bottled water on a bench,
bottled water for you.
    It's tempting to stay a child forever: no wars for you, no losses,
    nor the burden of autumn on your shoulders,
       the terrible season that tightens around your arm like a
           tourniquet.
Under a T-shirt erupts a crimson river
that irrigates our garden of confusion.

Next year new fruit will sprout and bloom,
But who will want to harvest them?


## Uneasy Evenings

these uneasy evenings come down on us from above,
but for you,
when the night is over you exhale the dust and the smog,
there's only the urge to sprout and bloom and jump over the spring and into the war.
to love is to listen to the sound of sirens, hugging each other,
and to hear the rhythms of the winds and imagine the movement of the planets,
and to see the deadly arch of enemy missiles and the scattering light of shrapnel,
and what lies between you and the bottom of the seas,
and to name what seemed forever unnameable,
and the way he's going to leave tomorrow for the eastern front,
and the way the current of silence leaves an almost invisible trace,
and the way March changes the course of rivers,
and the way the stars light up like lamps above someone,
and the way violins' camphor hardens inside you,
how every movement becomes heavier and every step deeper,
how someone's blood irrigates our fields,
how the land after rain steams with pain,
and all the martyrs and saints now bow over the soil,
and you embraced one another as if for the first time,
and the roads we travelled snapped like strings,
and the snow fell softly outside the windows,
and you had no strength
to leave
in these uneasy evenings,
that come down on us from above.

*Translated by Nina Murray*

POEMS
Kuli Kohli

## Child's Play

Playing on the streets with scabs on our knees,
scrapes on our elbows, our clothes soiled with
moss and grass with smears of dirt and mud.

We wrestle with each other, call each other
names, we fight, we squabble, we quarrel.
Instantly we forget and start playing again.

Our tantrums in fits of temper don't last.
Like clean sheets of paper, we are fearless,
where danger, threat, risk has no imprints.

We live in a cartoon world where everything
is joyous, looney, flamboyant, spellbinding,
in fairytales where the villains lose the plot.

Occasionally, we take notice of the grown-ups,
when they tell us off, nag at us and scold us:
'That's naughty! Why don't you do as we say?'

We watch, observe, listen, imitate our grown-ups,
only wishing to grow up faster than time allows.
We think of it as child's play. As easy as pie!

Years zoom by, suddenly we're in the adult world,
everything becomes a problem. Greed, envy, power
like thunderstorms, this world is grey and gloomy.

Pressures build and nothing is like it used to be,
we don't forget when time was like candy floss;
we wonder what on earth has happened to us.


## Mornings

After a night of thunder, heavy raindrops
fill the land with craters, where once happiness lived.
Our evenings used to be filled with fragrance of flowers,
where the moon and stars shone brightly,
but never descended upon us like alien comets.
The alarm of cockerels crowing and doves cooing,
we woke up refreshed like a running stream,
enticed by the morning breeze, we embraced and our love
showered us with gentle kisses.
This war of power and politics
has destroyed and deceived us like a python,
crushing everything it slithers around. And the poisons
we never tasted just keep spilling on us every day.
These mornings are dimmer than they used to be,
the neighbouring soldiers have upturned our homeland,
where darkness builds like a deep-sea monster
and tears us into a million fragments.
Our loved ones are gone, some gone forever.
We grasp onto our lasting lives,
our children who studied for their future
now train themselves with weapons and grenades.
Our blood boils but we still dance
taking things into our own hands,
we will fight until we win…
Just so our future can feel
those bright and beautiful mornings once again.

POEMS
Ihor Pavlyuk

## Mamai[1]

Battle.
It gets dark early.
Mamai's ghost is in the field.
He does not know how to die.
He is between hell and heaven.

Sometimes he sings, sometimes he fights,
Sometimes he laughs, sometimes he cries
Like a wounded bird,
The Cossack witcher.

Scars across him.
A seven-string sabre
Something in him is from God,
Something about him is from the crow.

And around, on the trees,
Disposable nests,
Styrofoam lions.
They drive Mercedes.
He is alien to this world.
He is stronger than it is.
His star is still shining

---

[1] Mamai: a mythical image of the Ukrainian warrior, representing the freedom and immortality of the Ukrainian people.

On the immortal road.
And people laugh,
And make their careers.

It's dark.
It is windy.
The ground is slippery.
The ghost of Mamai is in the sky.


## Sirens and Bells

These are not the sirens
That once awaited Odysseus.
You can't cover your ears with beeswax against their moans.
Tied to the mast, you will wait for the metal,
The blast wave of the diabolical depth.

These sirens are different...
And the war is not Trojan.
Although wars
Are all similar –
Like blood, –
Whether or not Ithaca is under attack.
Is Penelope waiting?
Europe?
Is Asia warlike?
The sirens of then and now
sing deadly similar songs.

When the All Clear sounds –
The sirens will stop.

Cathedral bells are heard
And the vertical flow of the Dnieper.

The enemy ship will go to...
The veins will expand.

The old era
Follows the tunnels of veins
To eternity.


## To 'The Brothers'

For pain – some vodka...
From this pain – a song.
And in the song – both shame and rebellion.
This is an abyss.
It's not too late to come here
Hearing God's trumpet.

I run like a dream
On white clouds
To my second childhood.
The apostles ran in tears...
Little faith.
Anguish.
And this aversion to poems.
Naked.
The words ring out stiffly.
Moscow brothers,
You are not a 'steppe horde'.
How to understand you?...

I you... and I you...
Well, what are you... creeps?...
I know, not an angel either...
They burned just as the Nazi did
My rural council
And talk about love.

You shoot us in the back
Satisfied and vile.

You have Poets!...

Sorrow flies on modern brooms,
It drinks bloody bad alcohol.

In seven generations
Someone will howl
About your fratricidal madness.
I know there are also people among you...
And I quietly feel sorry for them.

From pain – some vodka...
From vodka – a song.
And in the song – both shame and rebellion.
It's true.
It is not too late to come to the truth,
When you hear the sixth trumpet of God.

★ ★ ★

I'm ready to live,
I'm getting ready to die
For Ukraine,
A poet and a warrior...
Let them shoot
Heavy and stubborn –
But not in the back.

Brothers and sisters,
Ancestors and descendants,
Mum and Mamai,
And riot and magma,
The star and the field...

Everything in a circle.
Pain is not first.

Only fresh scars...

## The Fate of Humanity is Currently Wandering in Ukraine

Not in boundless space, not in a village cave –
In the cellars of Azovstal[2] is the fate of humanity today.

How far we've evolved after leaving the caves
To stand on the threshold of the end of the era!

We've replaced our cleavers and spears with missiles;
Lions, frogs, foxes lose their minds.

This is how a neighbour suppresses a neighbour, shows a bomb,
As if common sense is forever blocked by a blood clot.

Someone shouts, 'Putin is to blame!', someone does not like Trump.
The collective mind of humanity is a monkey with a grenade.

On the ruins of Azovstal in the City of Mary[3]
A deep crack divides memories and dreams.

The descendants of the Cossacks fight. Children die.
It's the Apocalypse. There is no escape from death.

Whoever comes with a rocket will die from the rocket.
Mariupol. The fate of humanity in the heart of Ukraine.


## From the cycle 'Spring and War'

3.

All wars are always beyond words.
Baghdad hums with the prayers of imams.
I, disappointed in humanity, have grown small,
Like a child under a bombardment without a mother.

---

[2] The Azovstal Iron and Steel Works, in Mariupol, eastern Ukraine. The plant was fiercely fought over during the Russian siege of the city in Spring 2022.
[3] Mariupol: 'City of Holy Mary'.

I've lost the voice of my one guiding star,
The voice I heard, like the ringing of my own blood in my ears.
The slave owners revolted –
The slaves,
They were always ready for anything.

The sadness is cosmic.
The slaughterhouse is still earthly.
Although not for land, not for honour...
If only...
War seeped into my spring,
Like a cowboy with the habits of a bandit.

So instead of birds above, planes,
Like silver crucifixes in gold...

Why doesn't humanity become human over time?
God Himself only knows.


## Human

My days became heavy and lonely.
I had thought – humanity is wiser...
Now my songs are quieter –
Eternal?
Are you a prophet?
I let them go, like my own children,
Like a baby bird.
Sweet autumn song, fly to God:
There is the homeland.

People are like people:
'Hosanna!'
'Crucify him!'
...People love the dead,
Not being able to live without war...
And not knowing how to live at all.

They won't be pleased,
No matter how I try.
It's better with cats.
The people of the golden era have passed,
They became cattle.

What's next –
Nobody knows.
Therefore I pray,
Comfort myself...

Human history,
Unfortunately, is war
Which will turn into Silence.


## Minefield

A bloody shadow on the minefield.
Poppies.
Cornflowers.
Wind.
On the belly of the minefield
Something moves, fur glistening.

Wounded by the light, birds fly,
They fly as if swimming, I swear to God.
And my brother Fox asks the way
from my sister River.

I forget plastic, the Internet.
I forget all the fuss.
I am small, small among the planets –
Like boats in summer.

From the body's bombshelter the dream's butterfly
Will fly to the star and melt.
The flowers of the minefield are old, very old

And sharp –
Like wounds of the soul.

And dogs like people
Wander sad.
Soldiers demine the distance.

We are not alone in the minefield.
But it's good that we are winged...


**Confession of a Spiritual Warrior**

I dreamed not what I wanted
Wounded in the soul through the back.
Hamlet mood...
A hundred devils
Want in me to make their homeland.

Death, in white, walked circles all around me.
I sipped silence with a crust of bread.
Banished devils a whip and a crucifix, out
To the winds that write a white song.

Heart these days is like a nest of crooks,
Cold and orphaned,
No one came to be here,
And the heart is not merely flesh.

Dreams are like memories.
Now
It's as if there hasn't been...
I don't feel.
I wrote a poem –
tore it...
Like a bag of golden tea.

Die – or sleep forever:

Is there a difference?
Is there any difference?
Tears well up.
Salty smoke
Sparkles with undaunted happiness.

Sin will flow into anger like mercury.
Sorrow – into joy,
And fire into water.

The spirit is immortal...

And for me it is an honour –
To die with my people...

Translated by the author

# THE PEOPLE-EATER OF LENINGRAD[1]
Sebastian Groes

A long time ago, before people were not quite human, there lived a couple in a slimy swamp that would one day become Leningrad. The land was ugly and hostile but the people were strong and good. After a while the woman fell pregnant. The swamp people were surprised as the woman was pregnant in two places: in her belly and in her thigh. When the time came, she first gave birth to a boy from her belly, and after that a boy was born from her thigh. The younger boy was just as sweet as his older brother and for a while the family lived in harmony.

Yet, after a few years, something happened that would change the family and village forever. For some inexplicable reason, the younger brother became jealous and greedy. He didn't want to share his toys and he started stealing food from his brother by inventing cunning ruses. In their shared bed, the younger one wrapped himself in their shared sheet, leaving his brother shivering in the cold. His large baby eyes shrunk to tiny piggy eyes and the full warm lips turned into a cruel stripe. He started making trouble all the time: he kicked and screamed whenever he didn't get what he wanted, he bit his older brother and beat his mother. The nasty little creep also smashed everything in their hut. Whereas his older brother was easy-going, the younger became a nightmare. He drove his parents and older sibling mad.

The village watched the family with bated breath. What would become of them? How would they keep the peace? They feared the madness would infect the entire township and everyone would stop making sense. What would become of humanity then?

---

[1] This story is an adaptation and translation of a fairy tale from Papua New Guinea mixed with references to Russian and Ukrainian mythology as well as the poetry by Ihor Pavlyuk in this collection..

For the villagers, the two children embodied two possibilities for their world. They symbolised two paths for the fate of humanity. On the one hand, there was the forward-looking and decent human being who came from the belly and, on the other hand, the selfish, discontented animal-man who came from the thigh. The difference between the two brothers soon became more and more pronounced.

The two boys continued to grow up in their soggy swamp. They hunted and fished, and learned the language of the animals, just like other children in that time. They spoke with the pigs and the birds. These people did not yet know how to make fire; meat was dried in the sun. There were no drums or guitars nor songs for pastime, so that people went to sleep early every night and dreamt of nothing but friendship and unity. They ate leaves and bark from trees. They also ate caterpillars, worms and insects. The villagers didn't mind this, as long as there was peace and harmony.

One day, when the brothers were just six years old, they were fishing in a creek not far from the village. They had gathered a bunch of shrimps and the older went into the forest to look for leaves in which he could wrap the shrimps to take them home. When he came back, he saw with astonishment that his brother was eating the shrimps alive. The poor beasts were writhing in his mouth, out of which ran trickles of pale blood. His eyes had rolled up into their sockets, leaving just the whites of his eye balls, which were covered in a web of throbbing red veins.

'What the hell are you doing?' his brother asked.

'Alive is more tasty than dead,' was his answer. From then on, the difference between the two boys became more and more clear.

When they were twelve years old, the two went hunting. They shot down creatures in the sky. When there are two hunters and their position to the target is equally favourable, then the rule goes that the elder needs to shoot the first arrow. As it should have been in this case. A fat bird sat in a tree and the boys were standing next to one another in an equal position. The elder was flabbergasted when his brother aimed his bow, shot the bird, picked it up and started to pluck it like a madman with the intention of eating it. The sky was full of feathers whilst the beast let out terrible, frightened cries of fear.

'Why are you shooting first?' asked the elder, outraged. 'You have violated the rules of our village.'

'Why wouldn't I shoot, older brother? I use my bow and arrow just as well as you. I am a warrior and I am not afraid of battle.'

Something similar happened when they were close to adulthood. In a cave by the river lived a big animal, a horrible looking creature, part man, part snake, part crocodile. It was a terrible monster, and its thirst for blood was insatiable. As long as this beast was alive, no one felt safe in the swamp land. This is why the brothers decided one day to kill the monster. They were lucky: they found the beast on its back, sleeping, its belly round. Carefully they crawled closer. This time the elder took aim but the younger snuck past him with two arrows on his bow and shot the hulking form of the monster. Blood spurted from its body.

'Why the hell are you shooting first?' asked the elder, annoyed.

'Because I have the guts to and I don't care about the rules,' said the younger, and moved towards the beast.

The monster wasn't dead yet. It raised his head and said, 'Before I die, I will give you some advice. Mark my words, they are very important.'

Reluctantly the brothers moved closer, afraid of the big body and the mouth with its terrible teeth.

But the monster only wanted to say the following: 'When you go fishing next time, work together to build a dam and scoop out all the water. This way you can catch all the fish. Further, you must leave your parents' hut and together build a grown man's house, invite your family and the villagers, and feed them aplenty. It must be a great feast. And, thirdly, you must think carefully about waging war with enemy tribes who mean you harm. When you are attacked in your village, you must stay if you're the strongest and run when you are weaker. But you must always try to avoid senseless battle.'

Thereafter a stream of blood spouted from the beast's body and it blew out its last candle. They brothers entered its den and snooped around. There were bones of humans and animals everywhere. The older brother tripped over a skull, which the younger brother started playing football with, laughing his mad laugh. In the back they heard tiny scared voices. They turned out to be the sound of two girls: the daughters of the monster. When they saw the men, they tried to run, but the brothers were quicker and caught up to them.

They saw that the girls were beautiful and mesmerising. They chatted to them. They all liked one another a lot. The boys thought the girls were kind and the women were impressed by the twins.

'This is great,' said the elder, 'now we can get married. I will propose to the older girl, and you to the younger.'

'Marriage will not be necessary,' answered the younger, 'as I will eat my girl anyway.' Thereon the younger chopped off her head, butchered her right then and there and put her flesh out to dry in the sun. He then also cut up the monster and put its meat out to dry. His white eyes rolled in their sockets as he ate the flesh of the one who was supposed to be his wife.

But the elder brought his bride home, built a grown man's house and invited all in the village to a party at which they ate aplenty. Everyone in the village was happy. Except for his brother, who couldn't understand why everyone was so merry.

For a while the brothers – the elder with his wife – lived together in their house. The woman had a child, a lovely baby girl. One day the younger brother said: 'We need leaves and bark to eat, would you mind getting some together with your wife?' His brother said yes and the next day departed with his wife and left their child with their mother.

But after being on the road for a while, he came to think about his sibling's unreliable nature, and returned home in great haste. His brother has already butchered and eaten his mother. Her flesh had been left out to dry on the stones in the courtyard.

'Where is our baby girl?' asked the older brother, grabbing him by the shoulders and trying to shake some sense into him.

'I ate her first. She was delicious, her meat so tasty and full of life. I couldn't help myself.'

The elder brother and his wife were deeply saddened. He took his bow and arrow and shot at his brother, but the younger shot back. So they shot at one another one day and one night until all their arrows were used up.

This is when they decided to talk. The elder said: 'Every time I see this house in which you ate our mother and child, I will think of your terrible behaviour. That will never change. We must part ways.'

'Yes,' the younger said, 'we must part ways. Before I eat you too. And your wife. And all the villagers. My appetite knows no bounds.'

'But, my brother, when you are at war,' the elder said in a

consolatory voice, 'you can count on me. Please reach out to me if you are in need of help.'

'I need no one, I am strong enough myself,' was his brother's reaction. He rolled his white-red eyes up his sockets and left his brother's house.

The elder went west, the younger east.

Today it is believed that in all likelihood it is from the descendants of the younger brother that the one-eyed Likho, causer of trouble and harbinger of death, sprang. The descendants of the elder brother brought forth the Mamai, the East European mythical warrior, the Cossack witcher, bringer of light, fire and order in society.

POEMS
Halyna Kruk


bifurcation point

in wartime Lviv – they would write later –
there was a vibrant literary milieu,
they probably published work as a group (just like *Mytusa*[1] once
    did)
or gathered for readings (what else can poets do in a war?)
so many of them here now:
*internally displaced* and *externally unstable*,
just like back in the day, briefly, during the wars one and two,
    heading to Europe,
before the iron curtain cut through modernity's horny nude body
yes, cutting right to the bone
although then one spoke more of Prague and Poděbrady, Warsaw
    and Munich –
but now too they would speak of Warsaw and Lviv,
Chernivtsi and Uzhhorod, Ivano-Frankivsk and Ternopil,
where so many of them were at once, those poets, that it seemed
that at any turn one could step into another one's poem,
into anxious dreams, history, the news, onto the same floor, sharing
    a mattress,
under the same handed-over quilted blanket
(what a brilliant metaphor for human coexistence in wartime –
but alas, already used by others!)
into one family, chipped and far from full...

---

[1] A monthly literature and art journal briefly published in Lviv from January to April 1922.

try explaining later to others that the first few months we met only by accident
only for business, for a couple of minutes, at times in the street, not recognizing each other at first,
shying away, as if recalling what's lost irrevocably, what's irretrievable,
hugging, instead of words, to hide the tearing eyes:
how are you – how are you – not a word about literature – hang in there – hang in there
silent and concentrated, just like the first Christians
who saw Christ's miracles with their own eyes and did not know yet
how to properly understand them, how to tell the others so that they would believe and not mock
how to not twist or muddle anything
for it is never clear which details are crucial, and which can be neglected
in each conversation we then diverged from what happened to us
like the apostles heading to different ends of the world, each preaching his own gospel
for every faith depends on millions of personal testimonies,
on countless private stories from that point in reality
where no one knows anything yet, or understands
what that man did to the dead Lazarus, and how he managed to do it,
and how all saw this but not all believed at first…
especially if it's a belief in victory from a point where it can't be seen yet at all
this is how they would write in a section about Ukrainian literature from the early 30s
the main thing is not to forget later that all of this was not at all about literature

# Brovary [2]

I've assigned myself tears
for a separate day
like a schoolchild
but it still doesn't finish
still doesn't finish


## surviving

that which preserves us from settling scores,
gives us strength to paddle though a February morning's cold waters,
exhaling a grey puff of steam, just like heavy smokers their puffs,
which prompts us to guess where is the closest shore
onto which sooner or later you could disembark, stand on firm ground
that which keeps us afloat, does not let us drown, pushes us out of the water
besides the Archimedean force and the Sisyphean labours,
besides subcutaneous fat and the desire to swim far, far away
in this deep worry that brings you to your senses and hurries you,
in this bittersweet despair that locks around your chest
forcing you to breathe in and breathe out
we are what we push to the margins of consciousness
into the chaotic visual stream of nightmares,
into the confusing childhood impressions that you can
neither recall nor forget,
that which we can't confess even to ourselves,
let alone to others, even when facing death:
we are hurried not by the strength but by the weakness
we always swim to the farthest shore
but this is learned only by those with sufficient
strength to swim to it, get out on dry land, look around,
accept as given

---

[2] A city in northern Ukraine.

that somewhere there, in the midst of these waters
where the bottom was in fact closer than the shore
(the bottom is always closer)
and the body already was giving up paddling, and the lungs inhaling
someone would replace us
and no one will notice the substitution

\* \* \*

young poets grow old so fast
as soon as they start noticing
language's scandalous pranks,
suspicious activity in the prefrontal cortex,
dopamine-dependency on words
the abyss behind the shoulders of the one
ready to make one step aside from oneself
the lightness of casual relationships
homonymy's *double entendres*
numbness in the tips of one's phrases
rhymed with far too much effort,
being far too attentive to artistic details
no one would remember later,
like who arrived with whom
and who was left with what
young poets grow old so fast,
most of them without even seeing
their first book
as if in poetry a year counts for two,
counts for a century, year after year,
something grabs your innocence,
your lightness and spontaneity,
mediocrity and genius
and from it you are left
only with crossed-out pages,
as if in someone else's hand
only shame from
how rosy, open,
naked, naïve

you arrived at the first poem
ready for anything
and you wanted to die
like after you first had sex
but then had to live on and on
live on, and on, and on
carrying from poem to poem
unneeded knowledge, extraneous experience,
tradition's withered body
once taken young by everyone
but no one wants to look after
its old age


**poem not about language**

so, you took over her language
which no longer tells me anything,
her logic of building phrases
that resembles woodworm's labyrinths
in the desiccated wood of an old cradle.
not every boat can become a cradle
so, you took over her voice
like it happens in a far too deep kiss,
when you hurt someone and become different
an alien hostile changeling
who would never again be able
to shed the animal skin.
love's skinned body is never white
it is pink with blue streaks,
more defenceless than dead,
mine, mine, you target what
you once focused your kisses on,
grabbed with your lips alone
like a berry off a branch that prickles all
except you. Not you, not for you
is this ripened acrid thought.
not you, not for you, you broke off

even if it seemed you were still holding that note,
but it no longer touches, no longer affects
in reality's swift-moving stream,
in soul's narrowest point,
in the tightness of a heart
when breathing slows
you can no longer swim through there


Dnipro, 14 Jan. 2023

in our home dangerous objects were always
hidden from children, all the various scissors and blades, needles and awls,
kitchen knives, into places hard to reach, into secret drawers
prickling and cutting, sharp and rounded, so that no one would get hurt
but who could have known how much danger there is
in an ordinary cast iron bathtub hanging above your head,
the collapsed wall of the living room, the nail from a painting
that holds in place the neighbours' apartment's ceiling
who could have known how heavy
the packed bookshelves can be, how hard the upholstered
furniture can be, our home is unreliable, our home is above an abyss,
our home's in the air full of scary voices
that cut to the bone, that pierce right through you,
that leave unhealable wounds
never before have they buried so many people at once in our home

★ ★ ★

Will I be able to make two steps forward, or will I stop here
next to the scattered bodies in unnatural poses
next to the rust of a burnt-out car that gapes with openings carved out by shells
that are too big to kill a specific person.
This is imprudent use of artistic resources, the world won't believe.

Lack of a logical motive, explain to me, says you, why are they killing us,
there must be some motivation, some reason.
They don't construct plots in books this way.
When you look from afar, there is always a chance to stop in time,
not to come too close, where the eye sees too much –
an ungainly broken nail on a well-cared-for woman's hand,
a child's slipper mixed with the rest of the apartment's contents.
Literature existed in order to convince
that a child's abandoned slipper is separate from the foot,
that a broken fingernail isn't much of a problem.
If you stop in time, don't get too close, don't look too close.
Safety distance, a barrier until which all this can still be
a banal thought-out plot, a forbidden fruit of the imagination overstuffed with catastrophism.
Literature is no longer a means for escape, only a reserved track
from which no one departs anywhere.
You board a train and understand – it won't help you, do you understand?
Sometime in the future you will de-mothball this path, in case of some urgent need,
you will remove the speed limit in this closed-off direction, allow yourself to see.
In the world where literature isn't for killing,
and isn't for settling scores,
and not for remembering,
and not for remembering all down to an iota,
when you don't want to see all this
under the rubble shown on the news, documented in photos.
This literature is worth nothing, do you hear me?
A child's slipper that slipped off a child and into the air
when they were mixed with fragments of glass and concrete,
a broken woman's fingernail on an arm under the rubble,
unblurred view of what has remained of the body,
a children's book on which you focus
not to see everything else,
not to imagine everything else
that was between the book and the hand,

between the moment of a family Saturday morning and the frame
    that came next.
You come too close – and you are pierced by the rods
of someone's muffled dying cry,
'I don't want to die.'
Literature lives on with this cry in your ears,
with this hand and this slipper,
knowing what was behind them in reality's unblurred version,
the version not softened by AI.
This is what literature has always been for.

                                        Translated by Vitaly Chernetsky

SPEAKING IN NEW TONGUES
Roy McFarlane

*A language disappears when no one speaks of love.* [1]


The language of conflict
the easiest of tongues to unravel

accents of pain, gibberish of slaughter
tones of dark skies flooding streets and basements

where poets grow old too quickly, writing
on the walls of homes that come tumbling down.

★

Oh, for the lyrics of love
found in a child's eyes
looking up into their father's voice
a voice drawn from realms of happiness,
words yet to be formed in their mouth
they know the language of love

because of the volume of the womb
they lived in hearing the sound of tenderness.

I pray in the wombs of conflict
children will know the difference

---

[1] Serhiy Zhadan, *How Did We Build Our Homes?* (translated from the Ukrainian by Virlana and Wanda Phillips).

between crying skies of artillery
and a mother's tears of love.

The difference between the bass of a bomb
reverberating and a father's voice calling their name.

\*

Sirens that rise from the plumes of
of grey smoke, call the names of those
trying to live day by day walking
under ash falling like snow.

In another time, Orpheus hearing
the voices of sirens, drew out his lyre
to play a louder tune, more powerful
than the beguiling sound of death.

So, let us draw lyrics and prose
to rebuild homes, where walls
can be scribed upon, echoing anew,
a language that we all can ascribe to.

FLOUR AND LIES
Liudmyla Taran

She can't quite get used to washing her mother's hair: she is bedridden and it's quite a chore, washing it in bed.

At night, Halyna keeps listening for her mother's breath: is she still alive? It is like it was with her children when they were small. She is all ears, her sleep thin, like a threadbare fabric you can see straight through.

A heart attack. So untimely. As if sickness or death is ever timely. The Xarelto is running out, along with myriad other medicines she had been prescribed – there's a pile of prescription slips. Where to hand them in now? Pharmacies are locked up, windows boarded. The country's at war.

Halyna has filled her windows with piles of books. A good reason to have collected them, it turns out. The windows are criss-crossed with tape and stacked with their spines. Perhaps this is what prayer would look like if it were made visible. The last roubles of her salary were always spent on books. Oh, the Silver Age; Anna Akhmatova, Tsvetaeva, Pasternak, Mandelstam. Is this it – 'The lie that elevates us?' And what about Fyodor Mikhailovich with his one small tear for a child? 'The higher harmony is not worth the tears of that one tortured child.' And who tortured our children, who killed them?

Lord, how things have turned out. Symbols all around. But this is not a novel. Not a film. This is war. A real war in real time. Happening to her, to all of us.

She feels like screaming in a strange, new voice. What about Svitlana, her granddaughters, Andriy? Her mother. Right, what to do about her hair? She remembered mum sending her as a little girl to check on her maternal grandmother on the other side of the village. The old woman, locked inside her body, lay near motionless on her iron bed. She couldn't get up without assistance. She'd ask little

Halyna, 'Would you comb my hair? I can't stand it.'

Like her own mother, her mother's sister barely had a chance: there were children, the work at the collective farm, vegetables, chickens, cows, rabbits, and of course her husband. She was run ragged. And grandma's unwashed head burned. She'd ask her granddaughter, 'Please, scratch it with a comb.' Under her pillow she kept a plastic comb with dense teeth. She would pull it out and offer it to Halyna. She didn't like combing grandma's hair, but what could she do?

She'd let out her grandmother's thin ponytail and comb it carefully. Then she'd prop her grandmother up on pillows and slowly run the comb from her forehead to the back. Grandma would sit there, withered, flat as a codfish, and she'd groan a little. The worst part was when she asked Halyna, 'When is death finally going to take me? When?' Halyna would turn to stone inside, wishing herself back home as hard as she could.

Her grandmother would half-close her eyes and sigh. Halyna was a dutiful girl. She kept combing. Dandruff would stick to the comb and she'd wipe it with a bit of flannel and keep combing.

Remembering this dandruff and looking at her window of prayer, Halyna recalls someone saying that you could wash hair with flour. Like back in the old Cossack days, when they didn't have water they washed themselves with dry clay.

'Call as soon as you get there.'

'Mum, how can I promise anything? Don't you know what's going on?'

Her daughter, with an enormous backpack, stands in the door. Her two children, frightened little birds, huddle around her. Halyna's tears run without words, and she no longer bothers to wipe them away.

'I will be praying for you. For Andriy. Lord keep you all –'

Abruptly, Svitlana silently makes the sign of the cross over her mother. Halyna has never known her daughter to make this gesture but she doesn't feel surprised. The door creaks as they shut it behind them; a small cry like a lost orphan thing. It has never made such a noise before.

She stands in the hallway and thinks about the journey her

daughter is about to take. About how she is unable to go with her. Evacuation. What kind of word is that? Refugees. What happens while they're on the road? Tanks have been on the outskirts of Kyiv before. Andriy – where is he now? Digging trenches? Did they even get automatic rifles? And ammo?

'Halynko?'
Her mother calls out to her, gently, the way she did when Halyna was little. The tenderness makes her want to cry out loud. The tenderness and the fear in the voice. The voice of a wounded bird. A dove. Mama, you are not allowed to die. Daughter, you are –
'Halynko?'
Mum's hair. Where was the flour?

Before the war, Halyna's sister was in a neurosurgery ward. While she sat with her, she remembered watching a nurse wash another patient's hair right there in bed: she had a collar-shaped trowel pan to fit around her neck and she moved her hands like a magician, swoosh-swoosh, lather, swoosh. The water ran into the pan and did not touch the mattress, which was inflatable, very expensive and anti-bedsore. At night, the compressor's light glowed bright green, and Halyna stared at it until her eyes closed. She slept lightly, drifting off between her sister's groans, each wakening like a needle through her heart.

*I'm so sorry, she is so beautiful.* People said this about her sister, many times, even when she had her head shaved, and a cap of bandages wrapped around it. And if she hadn't been beautiful – would they have felt less sorry for her? But Maria, even after such a difficult operation, was, indeed, beautiful, she was born that way. Halyna shuddered inside each time she heard these sorrys. Later, she heard a similar thing at the funeral of the man next door who had died at the front: 'He was so young... so handsome... Such a pity...'

Andriy, her son-in-law, is handsome too: tall, slim and strong, his eyes expressive and sharp like a falcon's. He had gone to the recruitment office on the first day and they had signed him up. Andriy had predicted this a long time ago, before 2014 even. Moscow would attack. The war is inevitable. Those people won't let us go free. They haven't changed since the times of Ivan the Terrible.

'Andriy, don't demonise Russia,' she'd said. 'It's the twenty-first century out there –'

'And they don't give a hoot. Don't you know your history?'

The conviction in his voice. Well, there it is now. Exploded. A full-scale war. On the twenty-fourth of February, in the twenty-second year of the twenty-first century, Kyiv shuddered with explosions. The Russians attacked on the same hour as the Nazis. This could only be a nightmare. But it wasn't. This was war.

A siren wails. An air-raid alert.

Go to what basement? What shelter? She couldn't very well drag her mother down there, could she? Let what comes, come – whatever is her lot. She was never a fatalist before, but now it seemed to make things easier. She wants to throw a window open onto the February cold and let the siren wail in, make it wail louder! Let it terrify them down to the marrow, to the smallest neuron, let it pierce their hearts like a thick steel needle.

When she was little, like all children, she was afraid of the dark. But in her fear there was an intuitive urge to plunge deeper into it, to leap into its maw out of her own volition: to meet it. She would step into a dark unlit room and speak through gritted teeth. 'Eat me, eat me now, big bad wolf!' The wolf lay in wait under the bed and could spring at her back at any moment. She'd dash into the corner of the room, slap her hand on the table, and dash back to the door. The wolf could not keep up with her. And she, intact and untouchable, would return to the brightly lit corridor, an inexplicable joy filling her entire being.

The siren wails on.

She goes upstairs and moves her mother gently, turns her onto her side, massages her back, rubs oil into her skin. God forbid she got bed-sores. Why is a bed-ridden person so heavy?

Afterwards she puts on a jumper, and another sweater on top of that, but she cannot get warm. Her hands are like ice. Her feet too. She must get warm.

A simple task: make some soup. Their pantry is well stocked for now: grains, salt, oil. A neighbour brought them a loaf of bread – she had spent half a day standing in line for it. The bread is what they call 'social bread', and Halyna is grateful. She used to buy more expensive kinds – 'Velvet' or 'Viennese' – as her mum could only chew the lightest, most airy bread, and even that very slowly. Halyna would pinch off bits of it for her. Feed her with a spoon like a child. Wipe her chin. The old are so like babies.

Yes, make some soup. She orders herself to do it, but she is sluggish, she feels as if her body keeps being torn into pieces and she is stitching herself together by the barest of threads.

A word surfaces in her memory: kintsugi. The Japanese art of repairing broken pottery. Translated, it means a golden patch or a golden seam: the cracked pieces of a beloved cup or plate are glued back together with a lacquer that has gold dust mixed into it. Where could she find a pinch of gold, or even the glue, to mend the cracks in herself, her own life? And to hell with her life. The entirety of Ukraine is cracking. What will happen to it?

The phone rings, the sound beating against the walls like a trapped bird. She dashes to it and grabs it with both hands.

'Svitlano... I was... Thank God. Has Andriy been in touch? Where is he?'

'Mum, everything's fine.' Her daughter's voice comes through as if from the bottom of a well. Is she in a shelter? Svitlano continues. 'Kateryna called. She is in Poland. She told me they brought children from Bucha to the local hospital. Girls and boys. They had been tortured. Had their teeth knocked out. Raped. They didn't say a word. Not a word. Mute children. Teenagers. The doctor, a Pole, came out of the room and couldn't look our people in the eye. He was in tears...'

'Why are you telling me this? Don't make me know...'

After her daughter hangs up she sits looking at the dark window. The windows are dark. Her soul is dark. But she has no right. Others have suffered so much more than she has. Stop. Despair is a sin. Mum, don't you dare die on me. Svitlana, save our children! Run to the ends of the earth if you have to, but they must survive. Or else who will be here on our land tomorrow? They say it openly: they're here to destroy us. The final solution to the Ukrainian question. Exterminate every last one of us. This is genocide. After wars, famines. Those who were not born in the 'forties did not have children in the 'sixties, and there were new souls from those in the 'eighties and 'nineties. And those who were born after independence are now being killed in the heart of Europe as the world watches. The world is 'alarmed and deeply concerned'. And so many of those who are at the front haven't even dreamt of having children yet.

She should sleep. Could she? She can hear a dog whining somewhere – not out in the street. Is it locked in an apartment somewhere? Abandoned?

Anxiety fills the air, makes nests in the corners and folds itself under the beds. Then it slithers out suddenly, and snakes around her feet. It is stuck, like a hair to her tongue. She reaches for her mouth, she feels like she's going to be sick. If only she could vomit this war, retch it out – retch out the dark bile and her innards' slime. If only she could erupt with this war.

She sits on the chair beside her mother's bed but does not turn on the telly – she is afraid to see terrible footage of cars pierced with bullets, buildings slashed apart, the black pennants of ash and burning rising from empty sockets that used to be windows. Her heart is racing. She needs to be twice as strong. To hold out. To survive.

If only she could sleep. Or just doze.

The apartment is crowded with strange people she has not invited. They are on the beds, on the couch, on the floor. There's nowhere to stand, everywhere she looks there are strangers. She chases them away, shouting, 'Get out! I didn't invite you!' They are silent but they do not move. Someone laughs at her pleading. Someone shoves her.

She opens her eyes. What a strange dream. Were those people refugees? Why then did she shout at them, try to chase them out? The entire country has been uprooted, they are all refugees now. Even the people who stay in their own apartments.

Her mother's breathing is too quiet. She gets up, bends over her and listens. Another siren. She just can't get used to them. The abandoned dog next door howls along with it. Halyna's cat hides under the bed. They'd better get used to this. This is going to last a while. This is war.

She goes to the corridor. They say it's safer to be between two load-bearing walls. She turns on the light above the mirror and sits down on a stool. Pulls out a pre-war magazine. The cover reads, 'Is Mariupol Ready for War?' She turns the pages.

A paragraph catches her eye. 'Evelyn has cut her teeth on the science of love. She has passed a master class in oral sex and a month-long course in sexual techniques. She is experienced in scripting bedroom role-play and an expert in the offerings of the adult-only stores.'

Halyna throws the magazine against the wall. She studies herself in the mirror. Her entire body is covered with red patches, like mange. Nerves? Nerves. Of course, what else? Why isn't Svitlana calling? She didn't promise to call every hour, did she? Andriy. Andriy. Where is he? What is happening to him?

You are not a rag. Pull yourself together. Pull every bit of yourself into a fist.

Try a meditation for the pituitary gland. Put a black dot on a piece of paper and glue it onto a wall. To meditate, you must sit directly in front of this dot and keep looking at it, without blinking, until you can no longer see it. Keep your eyes open as long as you can, but do not tense them. You may blink away tears.

She shuffles towards her bed. Maybe she can sleep a bit more. She sways like a stalk of seaweed.

She lies down and closes her eyes.

The steel-mirrored walls muddle her brain. She takes one turn after another – and finally she arrives. Amazingly, she has not lost her way in the maze of the bunker she had studied so long on the simulator. He is asleep. He had to be asleep: so much very particular logistical effort has been dedicated to this, so much diligent work of a whole chain of people. He sleeps, crumpled, like a pathetic homunculus, a wrinkled ancient embryo. She is filled with an endlessly revolted pity. Revulsion, the urge to throw up, but there was no hatred. The hatred that had burned in her all these terrible years now vanished like water into dry earth. Only revulsion. An ocean of revulsion. She has to complete her task.

She holds up the knife and strikes with all her strength. Long training on a mannequin had made the movement automatic. The blade went into his neck.

Blood spills as if from a toppled glass. It is black and as it spills it turns into black cockroaches, each with Putin's face. They swarm on the floor and the walls, climbing over her feet. Then the despair. But she had done what she had to do.

She awoke and looked around: where am I? What? What a dream.

It's getting grey outside. Morning is coming. Quietly, she decides to leave the apartment and go on the hunt for food. She'll stand in lines as long as she can. The Russian murderers shoot at people queuing for bread, for medicine, they bomb railway stations, schools, nurseries and theatres. These murderers have spent centuries choking us in their 'brotherly embrace'. Her friend Diana put it right in her Facebook post: 'The doctrine is, in fact, very simple. We must survive. Our enemies must no longer exist.'

The Bible does not say love those who murder you. They are not just enemies – they are murderers. But how terrible it is to hate someone all the time. You burn like a flaming torch, and you burn up. Curses bubble up from your chest. The ash of Klaas beats right next to your heart.[1] The ash that had been him. Not a trace of the person – just ash. No one could keep it together. They mine the people they killed. Monsters. Lord, why do you let this go on for so long?

I want the same to be done to them: they'll understand then, from inside their own skins. I want these sirens to bury them in basements and shelters and in the streets. I want their lives to pass in stinking lice-traps. I want them not to know where to run, where to hide. Have their buildings burst into pieces and burn right before their eyes. With them inside. And those who warn against the language of hate? They have not been in the trenches or at the front. They've not buried anyone in a coffin draped with the flag. Their children are alive and well, good and whole, not mad with fear.

Lord, deliver me from hatred.

Damp wisps of February morning light float in the air. There are people in the street. It feels better. I am not alone. Kyiv is still here. There are check-points: anti-tank hedgehogs, barricades, giant blocks

---

[1] In the Belgian writer Charles De Coster's 1867 novel *La Légende et les Aventures héroïques, joyeuses et glorieuses d'Ulenspiegel et de Lamme Goedzak au pays de Flandres et ailleurs* (published in English as *The Legend of Ulenspiegel and Lamme Goedzak, and their Adventures Heroical, Joyous and Glorious in the Land of Flanders and Elsewhere*) Ulenspiegel's father Claes is burned to death for heresy by the Spanish Inquisition. Soetkin, Claes's wife, makes a sachet containing some of his ashes, saying to Ulenspiegel as she gives it to him, 'Let these ashes, that are the heart of my man [...] be ever on thy breast, like the fire of vengeance upon the murderers.'

of concrete with armature sticking out, tall piles of sand. Young men in camouflage, stern and meticulous. They stop cars and check the papers. No one stops her. She wants to bow to these men, these boys. Tears fill her eyes. They are the ones who did not give up Kyiv. But Bucha, Irpyn, Hostomel, and the torn-up villages around them. Those photos: a man, shot, lying right in the street next to the bicycle; a woman's hand with red manicured nails in a muddy puddle; the bloodied children's book *Let's Learn to Read* in the shot-up car. Lord, how is this possible? For no reason at all. In our own land. Because we are Ukrainians? Genocide.

A woman walks across the street, pressing a baby close. What made you leave your house so early, where are you going? Why haven't you left for a safer place? The woman seemed to want to press the baby back into her warm womb, so it wouldn't hear the roar of the sirens, wouldn't know war.

The sirens' wail starts up again. People run to the underground pass, dash into the tube. The station is called 'Friendship of the Peoples'. Is this also about the 'brotherly embrace'?

Back in her apartment she leans over her mother. She's breathing. She's alive.

Against her best instincts, she checks Facebook and the news sites. She must know something.

In an official notice people are asked not to return to the capital: 'THE RISK OF DYING IN KYIV IS HIGH'. Lord, how many deaths.

The phone. Svitlana! The sound fills the room. She grabs it.

'Everything's fine. The children are okay. Andriy is alright.'

She can feel her breath, oxygen reaching her body for what feels like the first time in hours.

Svitlana is talking fast, full of news.

'Of course, he won't tell me where he is and what he's doing. But he called. The people in Lviv are saints. They welcomed us, warmed us up, fed us, and found us a place to live. We are making camouflage nets in the library. My girls will be all right here. Mum, do you remember my friend Maria? I brought her home a couple of times. She's from Horlivka. She's here. She's seen terrible things. She is twenty-five, and her hair is all grey.'

Halyna thinks of her own father's grey hair. The way he was when he came back from the war – he spent three years as a forced worker at a railway-car repair plant in Kassel and survived the bombing of Dresden. That's what they must do. Survive. Until the end of the war. But she should say, until victory. Because that is the only end now, it's victory or death.

Translated by Nina Murray

## MOTHER BECOMES DAUGHTER BECOMES –
Charley Barnes

This is important:
how the mother tends a dandruff scalp,
seeks medication though there is none;
observe how she shifts child from bed to basin.
These small tender acts, irrespective of war,
can show us what it means
to be mothered – othered – to be gentle
in a furious world.

In a furious world,
to be mothered – othered – to be gentle,
can show us what it means;
these small tender acts, irrespective of war.
Observe, how she shifts child from bed to basin,
seeks medication though there is none;
how the mother tends a dandruff scalp.
This is important.

LAST POEMS
Victoria Amelina

No Poetry

I write no poetry
I'm a novelist
It's just the war reality
devouring all punctuation
devouring the plot coherence
devouring coherence
devouring
As if shells hit language
the debris from language
may look like poems
But they are not

This is no poetry too
poetry is in Kharkiv
volunteering for the army


A Poem About the Poet's Death

when a poet is shot dead
readers ask his colleagues
can you please write a poem
about the poet's death?

the poem should start with love
maybe go through some rage

fear becoming fury
but in a couple of lines
inevitably return to love
love should always prevail
at least in poetry

the surviving poets listen
standing around the grave
like King Arthur's knights
thinking of the holy grail
of literature
having their words ready
like swords for love

and then something changes
another bombing begins
or it begins to snow
so silently
as if the world was written
only by the dead poet
and other poets have quit


### The Homecoming Story

When Mira left home, she took a bead from her jewelry box.
When Tim was leaving his town, he picked up a rock from the street.
When Yarka was leaving her garden, she took an apricot pit.
When Vira was leaving home, she took nothing.
I will be back soon, she muttered and took nothing at all.

Mira has grown a jewelry box from her bead;
she's growing a new home in the box.
Tim has started a city from his rock;
it looks just like his hometown,
except there's no sea.
Yarka has planted her apricot pit

now she has an orchard around it.
And Vira, who took nothing at all?
She is telling this story.

When you're fleeing your home, she says,
behind your back, it gets smaller to save itself.

Your home can turn into:
a grey rock,
a bead,
a last-year apricot pit,
even a Lego part,
a seashell from Crimea,
a sunflower seed,
a button from the dad's uniform.
When your home fits in your pocket,
then there it sleeps.

Now listen, you should pull your home out
in a safe place when you're truly ready.
Little by little, your home will grow,
and you'll never be homeless.
Remember, never.

So what did you take with you, Vira?

I took this homecoming story.
Here, I've pulled it out into the light –
little by little,
the story is growing.

> Translated by the author

NOTES ON THE CONTRIBUTORS

Victoria Amelina (**Вікторія Амеліна**) was born in Lviv in 1986. She was injured by a missile explosion during the Russian attack on Kramatorsk on 27 June 2023 and died on 1 July. Her published books include *The Fall Syndrome, or Homo Compatiens* (2014), *Somebody, or Water Heart* (2016), *Dom's Dream Kingdom* (2017) and *Stories of Eka the Excavator* (2021).

Ivan Andrusiak (**Іван Андрусяк**) born in Kosiv District in the Ivano-Frankivsk region, Ukraine, is a poet, children's author, fiction writer, translator and literary critic. In the 1990s he became a member of *New Degeneration* artistic group, and produced thirteen poetry collections. He is best known for his children's poetry and fiction: *Soft and Fluffy, Animal ABC, Bunny's Book, Lyakatsia, Stefa and Her Chakalka* and *Who's Afraid of the Bunnies?* The last won the Zolotyi Leleka Children's Literature Award in 2010. He was awarded the Lesya Ukrainka Literary Prize, the Smoloskyp Publishing House Prize, the Blagovist Literary Award, and the Corona Carpatica International Prize. He resides in the town of Berezan in the Kyiv region.

**Casey Bailey** is an award-winning writer, performer and educator, born and raised in Nechells, Birmingham. He was the Birmingham Poet Laureate 2020-2022. Casey's poetry has been published in a number of anthologies and journals, and he has issued three collections. As a playwright, he has brought plays to the stage in Birmingham and London, including *GrimeBoy,* which had a sold-out run at the Birmingham Rep. In 2022 Casey won a Royal Television Society award for a film for his poem 'Dear Brum'.

**Charley Barnes** is an author and academic. She teaches Creative and Professional Writing at the University of Wolverhampton. Charley's poetry has been published across literary journals, and she has also published several crime fiction novels as Charlotte Barnes. Her monograph, *Deconstructing True Crime Literature*, was published by Palgrave Macmillan in September 2023.

**Tetiana Belimova** (**Тетяна Белімова**) is an award-winning writer, poet and novelist, born in Kyiv, Ukraine. She received her doctorate in Philology from Taras Shevchenko Kyiv National University, where she teaches Ukrainian Literature. Tetiana is a laureate and winner of International Literary Contest 'Coronation of the Word' for the novels *Kyiv.ua, Free World, Guilty People* (followed by a sequel, *Other People's Fault).* She is a fellow of Ministry of Culture and Sports of Austria for the creative project *Refugee: Notes on the Fields of War,* 2022.

**Anthony Cartwright**'s fiction centres on the lives of working-class families in the English West Midlands. His work has been featured on BBC Book at Bedtime, shortlisted for the Gordon Burn Prize, the James Tait Black Memorial Award and the Commonwealth Writers Prize, and been the recipient of a Betty Trask award. He was a secondary school English teacher and a writer-in-residence in inner-London schools as part of the First Story project. He currently teaches on the Creative and Professional Writing degree at the

University of the West of England, Bristol, and lives with his family in Cardiff.

**Vitaly Chernetsky (Віталій Чернецький)** is a Professor of Slavic Languages and Literatures at the University of Kansas. A native of Odesa, Ukraine, he received his Ph.D. from the University of Pennsylvania and has been translating poetry and prose into English since the mid-1990s. His translations into English include Yuri Andrukhovych's novels *The Moscoviad* (2008) and *Twelve Circles* (2015) and a volume of his selected poems, *Songs for a Dead Rooster* (2018, with Ostap Kin), a book by the Ukrainian artist Alevtina Kakhidze, *Zhdanovka* (2006), two children's books by Romana Romanyshyn and Andriy Lesiv, *Sound* (2020) and *Sight* (2021), and *Winter King*, a poetry collection by Ostap Slyvynsky (2023, with Iryna Shuvalova). His translation of Sophia Andrukhovych's novel *Felix Austria* is forthcoming from Harvard University Press.

**Carmel Doohan** is an author and academic. Her debut novel, *Seesaw*, was published by CB Editions in 2021. She has a Ph.D. from the University of Glasgow and is a visiting lecturer and writer-in-residence at the University of Wolverhampton. She is currently working on her second novel.

**Sofiya Filonenko (Софія Філоненко)** was born in Berdyansk, Zaporizhzhia region, Ukraine. She is a doctor of philology, and professor at the Ukrainian Catholic University, Lviv. She received her doctorate in Literary Theory from the Schevchenko Institute of Literature, National Ukrainian Academy of Sciences. Her research fields are Popular Culture, Popular Fiction, and Gender Studies. She has published three monographs and over 160 articles in Ukrainian, Polish, Georgian, Mexican, Romanian, Croatian, American and Spanish journals.

**R. M. Francis** is Senior Lecturer and Programme Leader for Creative and Professional Writing at the University of Wolverhampton. His novels *Bella* (2020) and *The Wrenna* (2021) were published by Wild Pressed Books, and his poetry collection, *Subsidence* (2020) by Smokestack Books. He co-edited the book *Smell, Memory and*

*Literature in the Black Country* (Palgrave Macmillan, 2021). In 2020, he became poet in residence for the Black Country Geological Society and produced his book of poems and essays *The Chain Coral Chorus* (Playdead Press). His collection of horror stories, *Ameles / Currents of Unmindfulness* (2023) is published by Poe Girl Publications.

**Niall Griffiths** is an award-winning writer of novels, short stories, poetry and various non-fiction works including articles for *The Guardian* and the BBC. He lives in mid-Wales. His most recent novel is *Knotted*, published by Repeater Press in 2023.

**Sebastian Groes** is Professor of English Literature at the University of Wolverhampton, where he is Director of the Centre for Transnational and Transcultural Research. He is Principal Investigator of the Arts and Humanities Research Council-funded Novel Perceptions: towards an inclusive canon. His first non-fiction book, the stroke memoir *Right in the Head*, was published by Jetstone in 2023. He has published various short stories in English and Dutch, is working on a novel, whilst developing an online creative writing tool for people with acquired brain injury.

**Kerry Hadley-Pryce** is a British writer and academic. Her first novel, *The Black Country* (Salt, 2015), came out of her M.A. in Creative Writing at Manchester Writing School, for which she won the Michael Schmidt Award for Outstanding Achievement. Her second novel, *Gamble* (Salt Publishing, 2018), was shortlisted for the Encore Second Novel Award in 2019. Her third, *God's Country*, was published by Salt in 2023. She has had short stories published in various anthologies and online by Fictive Dream and The Incubator. Her short story 'Chimera' was republished in the *Best British Short Stories 2023* anthology. She has a Ph.D. (on 'Psychogeographic Flow in Black Country Fiction') from Manchester Metropolitan University and teaches creative and professional writing at the University of Wolverhampton. She is working on her fourth novel.

**Kuli Kohli** was born with cerebral palsy in India. She now lives in Wolverhampton and is married with three children. She retired from Wolverhampton City Council after working there for thirty-two years.

She runs the Punjabi Women's Writing Group. Her poetry volumes *Patchwork* and *A Wonder Woman* (2021) are published by Offa's Press. She has performed at universities in London, Berlin and Liverpool, and at the British Museum in London. She was appointed Poet Laureate of Wolverhampton from 2022 to 2024, and was awarded an Honorary Doctorate by the University of Wolverhampton in 2022. She writes for Disability Arts Online and is involved in various projects around the UK. Recently, she completed a commission for the National Portrait Gallery on a project called UK Citizen Wolverhampton: Punjabi Migration Experiences, which was exhibited at Wolverhampton Art Gallery in June 2023.

**Bogdan Kolomiychuk (Богдан Коломійчук)** is a Ukrainian novelist and short story writer born in Khmelnytsky region and living in Lviv. In 2002-2010 he worked as an actor and artistic director's assistant for the First Theater in Lviv. His novel *Ludwysar: The Games of Noblemen* won the Grand-prix of International Literary Contest 'Coronation of the Word' (Kyiv) in 2012. He was a co-founder and curator of the cultural project 'Carpathian Literary Residency', 2017-2018. His biography about a composer and music teacher from Lviv, Franz Xaver Mozart, was supported by the International Classical Music Festival 'LvivMozArt', and won the prize for the best novel in 'The City' category of the Lviv Book Forum 2018. Since February 2022 Bogdan has been a sergeant in the Armed Forces of Ukraine.

**Halyna Kruk (Галина Крук)** was born in Lviv. She is a poet, fiction writer and translator. She holds a Ph.D. in Ukrainian Literature and is currently researching in Ukrainian baroque literature at the Ivan Franko National University in

Lviv. Kruk is the author of five books of poetry, *An Adult Woman* (2017), *Co(an)existence* (2013), *The Face beyond the Photograph* (2005), *Footprints on Sand* and *Journeys in Search of a Home* (both 1997), the collection of short stories *Anyone but Me* (2021), and four books for children. In 2003 she won the Step by Step international competition for children's books. Her works have been translated into more than twenty languages and published in various poetry collections, magazines and anthologies in many countries, including the U.S., Poland, Lithuania, Germany, Sweden, Denmark, the Czech Republic, Italy, Estonia, Norway, Colombia, and China. In 2017-2019 she was a vice-president of the Ukrainian PEN.

**Roy McFarlane** is a poet, playwright and former youth and community worker, born in Birmingham of Jamaican parentage, living in Brighton. He is the National Canal Laureate, a former Birmingham Poet Laureate and one of the Bards of Brum, performing in the Opening Ceremony for the Birmingham Commonwealth Games in 2022. His debut collection, *Beginning With Your Last Breath*, was followed by *The Healing Next Time*, shortlisted for the Ted Hughes award and longlisted for the Jhalak Prize. His third collection, *Living by Troubled Waters* (Nine Arches Press), was published in 2022.

**Rostyslav Melnykiv (Ростислав Мельників)** is a poet, researcher and professor at H. S. Skovoroda Kharkiv National Pedagogical University, Ukraine. He is the author of several poetry collections: *Deer Hunting* (1996), *Journey to the Equinox* (2000) and *Steppe Apocrypha* (2016). Several non-fiction works include the monograph *Mike Johansen: Landscapes of Transformations* (2000). His poetry has been translated into English, Bosnian, Italian, German, Polish, Russian, Slovenian, and Czech.

**Nina Murray** is a Ukrainian-American poet and translator. She is the author of the poetry collections *Glapthorn Circular* (LiveCanon Poetry, 2023) and *Alcestis in the Underworld* (Circling Rivers Press, 2019) as well as several chapbooks. Her award-winning translations include Oksana Zabuzhko's *Museum of Abandoned Secrets* (Amazon Crossing), and Oksana Lutsyshyna's *Ivan and Phoebe* (Deep Vellum).

**Ihor Pavlyuk** (Ігор Зиновійович Павлюк, sometimes transliterated as Ihor Pawlyuk, Igor Pavlyk, or Igor Pavluk), born 1 January 1967 in Rozhyshche Raion, is a writer, translator and researcher. He was named the People's Poet of Ukraine in 2020. He is the winner of a 2013 English PEN Award, and the winner of the Switzerland Literary Prize 2021. He also holds a doctorate in Social Communication. Pavlyuk is a member of the English PEN and member of the European Society of Authors.

**Dmytro Semchyshyn (Дмитро Семчишин)** is a poet, literary theorist, and translator. He was born in 1990 in Omsk, Russia, to a Ukrainian family which returned home in 1992. He has a Ph.D. in Literary Theory from Petro Mohyla Black Sea National University in Mykolayiv, Ukraine. Dmytro worked as a teaching assistant at this university and as a librarian at the public libraries. He translates poetry from English into Ukrainian. His works were published in the Ukrainian literary magazines *Dzvin*, *Kyiv*, *Vsesvit*, and online. Some of his poems were translated into German and appeared in *Orte* (Schwellbrunn, Switzerland) and *Ostragehege* (Dresden, Germany).

**Liudmyla Taran (Людмила Таран)** holds her M.A. degree from Taras Shevchenko Kyiv National University. She has published six collections of poetry, nine collections of short stories and seven books of non-fiction (interviews, essays, literary criticism) in Ukraine, Australia, Great Britain, Canada, Lithuania, Poland, the USA, and the Czech Republic. She is a member of PEN Ukraine and the National Writers' Union of Ukraine. Liudmila was awarded the Oleksandr Biletsky award for literary criticism (1996), the Vasyl Mysyk (1996) and the Yevhen Pluzhnyk (2005) awards for poetry, and the UN Program Gender in Development award for journalistic and social activism (1998).

**Roksolana Zharkova (Роксолана Жаркова)** (Lviv) is a Ukrainian writer, essayist, and literary scholar, with an advanced degree in philological sciences. She is a feminist and a researcher of women's writing. She graduated from the Philology Department of Lviv National Ivan Franko University. Zharkova has been a participant, finalist, and winner of many national and international literary contests, and a laureate of several literature awards. She is the author of poetry collections *LISten – the Sea: Just Poems* (2015), *With Hands and Words* (2017) and *All My Birds* (2019), as well as a collection of novellas and short stories, *He Smells of You* (2017). Her debut novel, *Zero Point Zero* (2021), won the fifth national Hryhor Tyutyunnyk literary contest and was named by the Ukrainian PEN Club one of the best books published in Ukraine in that year. Zharkova's writing is often about women's traumatic experiences; it touches on the themes of war, trauma, migration, refugees, and the problem of borders in literature and art.

# Acknowledgements

The editors would like to thank, first and foremost, the Ukrainian writers and translators who contributed to this book: you have been writing about horrible events under extremely difficult, traumatising circumstances. We cannot thank you enough for giving us this multi-perspectival, diverse insight into your experiences. Please be assured that we will stand by you, unwaveringly, and that we will work and, at some point, celebrate together in a brighter, post-conflict future which will eventually come.

We wish to thank the translators, Vitaly Chernetsky and Nina Murray, for their work. We especially thank Vitaly for also providing the brief introduction to the literary history of Ukraine. Another special Thank You goes to Professor Sofiya Filonenko, who coordinated and liaised with the Ukrainian authors under difficult, often dangerous situations. We must pay special tribute to Victoria Amelina, whose death by a Russian missile strike means a loss for writing communities across the globe.

We thank the Black Country writers who gracefully declined any compensation for their wonderful contributions to this special book. Your generosity is much appreciated.

We thank the Centre for Transnational and Transcultural Research (CTTR) at the University of Wolverhampton for financial support. CTTR's aim to connect with and understand other cultures is one that is incredibly valuable during these times of polarisation and we hope to be able to continue to contribute to intercultural dialogue. We also thank the Being Human Festival – Amanda Phipps, Rose De Lara and Mark Johnson – for funding and promoting our events so generously. We also need to thank the financial backers of the Being Human Festival: the School of Advanced Studies; the British Academy; and the Arts and Humanities Research Council.

The British editors are grateful to their wonderful colleagues working in the Humanities at the University of Wolverhampton for their support in trying times. We also express our gratitude to the staff and students at Berdyansk State Pedagogical University for our collaboration and their contribution to the 'Positively Disruptive' Being Human Festival event in November 2022.

Printed in Great Britain
by Amazon